**Books should be returned on or before the
last date stamped below.**

MELDRUM MEG WAY, OLDMELDRUM

Sillars, Ravey

Strangers in Achnacraig

F

1130928

STRANGERS IN ACHNACRAIG

Brian Hamilton's wife, Fiona, was only twenty-six to his forty-two, but their three-year-old marriage had only served to deepen their love. Brian had recently retired from the Navy and they had just moved to a little croft on the coast at Achnacraig in the West of Scotland. Brian was hoping the fresh air there would be good for Fiona as she had acute asthma. When Fiona tells Brian she is expecting a baby, he is very concerned; she has defied the doctor's orders and put herself at risk. Who could tell what price they would have to pay?

Books by Ravey Sillars
Published by The House of Ulverscroft:

THEIR ISLAND OF DREAMS

RAVEY SILLARS

STRANGERS IN ACHNACRAIG

Complete and Unabridged

ULVERSCROFT
Leicester

First published in Great Britain

First Large Print Edition
published 1999

F

1130928

Copyright © 1988 by Ravey Sillars
All rights reserved

British Library CIP Data

Sillars, Ravey
    Strangers in Achnacraig.—Large print ed.—
Ulverscroft large print series: romance
1. Love stories
2. Large type books
I. Title
823.9'14 [F]

ISBN 0–7089–4113–3

Published by
F. A. Thorpe (Publishing) Ltd.
Anstey, Leicestershire
Set by Words & Graphics Ltd.
Anstey, Leicestershire
Printed and bound in Great Britain by
T. J. International Ltd., Padstow, Cornwall

This book is printed on acid-free paper

'Take Care, Darling'

Westering home, and a song in the air . . . '
Brian Hamilton's voice rose joyously as
they drove through the Highland glen. All
about them the mountains towered. Streams
hurtled down their steep sides and plunged
into the river, which tumbled and foamed
along beside the road.

'Great, isn't it?' Brian commented, turning
to his wife, Fiona, who sat beside him in
the van.

'It's terrific! So many contrasts. All this
grandeur after the peaceful hills of the last
stretch. And just look at these white shores
on the loch.'

'I know! And all this water! How many
lochs have we seen?' Brian queried.

'Oh, about six or seven, now, I'm sure.'

'I wish we could share some of our water
with the countries that have too little!'

Fiona looked at her husband and her
face became a little dreamy. People often
made that kind of remark lightly, but Brian
genuinely cared about others . . .

After the many miles of magnificent glen,
they found themselves driving by the side of

1

yet another loch. The landscape had softened again. The hills were now grassy slopes, patched with dark green pine forests.

'I think the West of Scotland must be the loveliest place in the world!' Brian declared.

'I shouldn't be surprised!' Fiona smiled tenderly at her husband's enthusiasm. A quiet happiness pervaded her, temporarily dispelling her doubts about moving to such a remote area. It was going to be lovely having him beside her all the time — now that he'd retired from the Navy.

She looked out at the glittering water of the loch, the blue sky and white clouds reflected in it. It was a perfect day, and the mood set Brian singing again.

'This is my lovely day . . . ' His pleasing baritone took up her thoughts and she laughed delightedly.

He finished his song with an exaggerated operatic flourish.

'We shouldn't be more than an hour and a half, now, dear,' he said. 'Not too tired, are you?'

'No, I'm fine,' Fiona answered him.

In truth she was a little tired, but wouldn't have let Brian guess for the world.

He chuckled and seized her hand, squeezing it lovingly.

'Packing up was an exhausting business.

Why not try to sleep for the rest of the way?'

'And miss all this glorious scenery . . . '

It was late afternoon and they'd been driving since mid-morning. In the hired van, they were heading for the Highland croft they'd purchased on the coast at Achnacraig.

'Married to a serviceman for three years, I should be used to moving!' Fiona said with a smile. She picked up Sam, a lucky mascot which sat between them on the seat. Sam was a teddy-bear dressed smartly in a sailor's suit and a Naval cap. He was a parting gift to Brian from his mates at the Naval base.

'Nice little chap, isn't he?' Brian grinned, glancing at Fiona holding Sam, like a child, in the crook of her arm.

'Mmm . . . '

'Think we should get him a kiddie's car seat?'

The remark was innocently lighthearted, but it hurt Fiona momentarily. Then, not wanting to spoil the happy atmosphere, she rallied her spirits.

'Yes. Let's!' She laughed. 'Oh, Brian, it's going to be lovely having you with me all the time! Just you and me and Sam at Rowanlea! I used to hate it when you were away at sea!'

'I know. But nothing's going to separate

us now. We're going to be deliriously happy. You'll see. For I'll go no more a-ro-o-ving without you, fair maid . . . ' he sang happily.

★ ★ ★

The sea shanty over, Brian was keeping his eyes on the road. Fiona had gone rather quiet. She'd be tired, he thought, although she wouldn't admit it. She was full of pluck and he was glad he'd managed to get his retirement from the Navy.

Fiona was only twenty-six to his forty-two, but their three-year-old marriage had only served to deepen their love. Life in Achnacraig was going to be all he had dreamed of for them. He couldn't wait to get there!

After the burst of song, Fiona had drawn in a deep breath and found that she couldn't quite complete it. She sat very still, trying not to make any more sound.

Brian suddenly became aware that Fiona's hands were trembling and that she was breathing with difficulty. He looked at her and saw her face had gone ghostly white.

'Are you all right, darling?' His brown eyes were filled with concern as he pulled the van off the road. 'Why didn't you tell me? Where's your bag?'

Fiona was too distressed to speak. She was gasping for breath.

Quickly he found her bag in the glove compartment, pulled out her inhaler and held it for her as she gratefully breathed in the healing vapour and tried to relax.

She was very pale now and her heart was pounding. He slipped his arm round her shoulders and held her as she leaned against him.

'Poor darling! Just relax. Stay calm.' He held her and patted her. 'We'll rest here for a while.'

'Oh, Brian, why did I have to develop asthma?' she asked when she could speak again.

'I don't know, dear.' His eyes were full of loving kindness and sympathy. 'Maybe it runs in your family.'

'Perhaps — but there's only two left to ask — Uncle Hugh and Aunt Ethel. They'd know, I suppose, having brought me up since my parents died. Still, they never mentioned asthma in all the years I stayed with them in the Borders.'

'I'm sure it was the strain of moving that brought on that attack. The quiet, peaceful life is what you need.' He pulled her against his shoulders and put his head down on hers.

5

She was infinitely precious to him. It would destroy him if anything happened to her.

'I love you so much,' he murmured.

Fiona turned her face up to look at her husband, his crisp brown hair, tanned skin and warm, peat-dark eyes.

'And I couldn't live without you . . . '

'Hush. You're going to get better in Achnacraig. It's exactly the kind of spot Mr Evans, the specialist, insisted on.'

'On the Gulf Stream!'

'On the Gulf Stream. Mild all the year round. Well, if you don't count the occasional nasty winter, that is. And, not only that — it's peaceful and quiet and out of the way.'

'The perfect sort of place to bring up a baby . . . '

'Come on, Fiona,' Brian said softly. 'We've been all through that. You know Mr Evans said we won't be able to start a family for some time. The strain on your heart . . . Try to be patient, dear.'

★ ★ ★

When they resumed their journey, Fiona quietly watched the terrain change again, as she waited for her pulse to return to normal. They soon turned into a road that was only single track with passing places, bordered on one side by a pine wood.

Further on, oak and beech trees made a tunnel of the road and then rhododendron bushes, coming into bloom, rose in tiers to an astonishing height on a cliffside. The gorse, massed behind the ditches, had already exploded into dazzling yellow flame.

'It's all so lush and fertile!' Brian's spirits spiralled upwards again as a blue sea-loch opened out below them, one of the long arms of the Atlantic cradling the rugged hills.

Where the loch widened to meet the sea, the road dropped down into Achnacraig. Across the water they could see the other shore and, away out to sea, the mountains of the Inner Hebrides rose smokily against the sky. The clouds had turned pink now and cast a rosy glow over the Sound, partly hidden by a horn of land that protected the village from the western breezes.

'Nearly home now, darling. Nearly home!' Brian's voice caught as he took in the lovely serenity of the scene. 'Are you feeling better now?'

Rather wearily, Fiona nodded her acknowledgement.

In the back of the van the few pieces of furniture that they owned were secured, along with their other possessions. Brian had collected various tools and implements, rolls of wire netting, sacks of seed potatoes, bags of grain and a wheelbarrow.

'It's still a bit rough and ready — the house . . . ' he said hesitantly.

'Oh, don't worry! We'll manage!' Fiona said.

'You're a game one!' Brian flexed his fingers on the wheel. 'The keys are at Miss Macpherson's at the schoolhouse. Just as well we arranged for you to stay there tonight. She's a wonderful lady. I'm sure you'll like her.'

'That's good. Look, Brian, don't say anything to her about my asthma. I don't want her to think I'm on my last legs or anything. First impressions and all that . . . '

'Fair enough, love. I understand,' Brian replied softly.

He left Fiona sitting in the van and walked up the short gravel drive to the grey-stone house attached to the school building.

Julia Macpherson threw open the door with a welcoming smile. She was a well-built, pleasant-faced woman in her mid-fifties with grey wings forming in her ash-brown hair. Intelligent hazel eyes sparkled at Brian as she opened the door wider.

'Come in, Brian. Dougal left the keys for you and I've bought in a few groceries I thought you might need for the weekend.'

'Thank you, Miss Macpherson!' Brian gave her a wide smile of appreciation. 'I hope Dougal managed to get the new panes into the porch windows.'

'Oh, yes, I think he did. Don't stand out here. Come in!' She entered. 'Where's this wife of yours then? I've been longing to meet her.'

'Well, she's out in the van. Actually she's a bit tired after the journey and she's anxious to see Rowanlea. You don't mind if we take a run up there first before I drop her overnight things off?'

'Of course not,' Julie replied. 'You'll both be anxious to see the place. But what about you, Brian? You must be tired, too. Are you still determined to stay in the croft tonight?'

'Oh yes, I'd better. That way I'll be able to get the van unloaded, ready to take back in the morning.'

'Well, I'm sure we could fit you in here if you change your mind. Now, come on, I'll introduce myself to your good lady.' Impetuously Julia was out of the door and hurrying down the path before Brian could turn around.

Her first impression was that Brian Hamilton's wife was very pretty. Dark, softly-waving hair tumbled about a heart-shaped face. The bone structure was fine and there were well-marked eyebrows above huge eyes — thickly fringed with black lashes. But she seemed very pale and wan.

'Hello, dear. I'm Julia Macpherson. Welcome to Achnacraig.' Julia poked a hand through the open window. 'Please come in. I'm going to make some tea for you.'

'Oh, that's very kind of you!' Fiona smiled with a forced brightness. 'But . . . I don't know if we should stop. We've such a lot to do!'

'Oh, do come in,' Julia coaxed. 'You must be weary. It's many a long mile from Glasgow.'

The woman's generosity and kindly manner appealed to Fiona and she decided to accept the invitation, even though she still wasn't feeling too good.

'Actually, I'd love a cup of tea!' Fiona slid down from the passenger seat rather stiffly.

The schoolhouse sitting-room had a comfortable, lived-in appearance. A solid table was covered with books and open jotters as though they'd interrupted Miss Macpherson in the middle of correction.

There was a bookcase, crowded with books, on one wall, a bureau on another, and a chintz-covered settee and easy chairs were invitingly arranged round the fireplace.

Julie bustled off into the kitchen and Brian turned to Fiona.

'How are you feeling now, love?' he asked.

'I'm fine. Just a bit tired — don't worry about me.'

They could hear the clatter of cups and Brian drifted off to carry the tray in for Miss Macpherson.

'Just call me Julia,' she told them, coming in with the teapot. 'Miss Macpherson's such a mouthful, and it makes me feel like the village school mistress — which I am, of course!' She laughed a deep, melodious laugh. 'Brian remembers me when I was in my thirties and he was about fifteen, but the gap seems to get narrower as you get older!'

★ ★ ★

While Fiona sat quietly enjoying her tea, Brian was regaling Julia with a colourful account of their journey.

'Oh, it's great that you're coming here to stay,' Julia said, warming to Brian's vibrant personality. 'You're just what we need — more young folk with their lives before them. It's so sad to have the community shrinking and so many of the houses just

11

used for holiday homes.'

'It'll still be busy in summer, like it used to be, though?'

'Oh, yes. More than ever now. Tourists, especially motorists, call, and a good number of yachts come in. Some of the crofts do bed and breakfast . . . ' She was interrupted by a knock on the outside door.

Then they heard it open and a voice calling.

'It's me — Eileen! May I come in?'

'Come in, Eileen!' Julia called back, smiling and rising to greet her guest.

The door of the room opened and a girl stood, hesitantly, framed in it.

'Sorry! I did see the van outside — and I wondered if you might have company. I'll come back another time. Here's the jumper pattern you wanted . . . ' She stepped forward and laid the paper on the table. 'I found it at last.'

'Don't go away.' Julia stretched out her hand to her. 'Come and meet Mr and Mrs Hamilton who've taken Rowanlea. You won't remember when Brian came here as a boy. This is Eileen McArthur,' she told them.

'How do you do?' Eileen came forward with her arm outstretched and shook hands with them. Her voice was soft and low pitched. It had the west-coat music in it and

12

the clearest diction Fiona had ever heard. It was a pleasure to listen to her.

'I know your father,' Brian told her.

Eileen accepted a chair and a cup of tea, seating herself with a natural, shy grace, her long legs neatly tucked to one side. She wore a skirt of an off-white tweed mixture and a toning Fair Isle sweater. There was a pleasing unity about her appearance. With her fair hair and deep skin tones, she made a restful presence in the room.

She listened carefully as Brian outlined some of his plans for the croft, only interrupting when she had a helpful suggestion to make.

Before she left she told them they must come to the ceilidhs that were held almost every week in the village hall.

'If there's anything I can help you with,' she added, 'if there's anything you want to know, our house is just three along from the school.'

After she'd left, Brian looked anxiously at his wife.

'We'd better be getting along to Rowanlea.'

'Oh.' Julia jumped up. 'I've got that milk and bread and things for you here, I'll just get them.' She made for the door.

'Are you awfully tired, darling?' Brian asked his wife anxiously. 'We won't stay too long at the croft . . . '

'I'm OK — honestly! Stop fussing,' she chided gently.

* * *

Rowanlea was a neat, squat, little cottage with two windows, which Brian had had enlarged, on either side of a glass porch, and two outshot windows above, peering from the slate roof.

They went into the room on the right of the central passageway. It was a good-sized living-room, but it was rather bare and untidy looking. There were wood-shavings on the floor where some carpentry had been in progress. Paint tins, buckets and brushes stood on the floor under the window and rolls of wallpaper lay on the table in the middle of the room.

Brian pressed a switch and a feeble light appeared, doing little to enhance the scene.

'I'll have to get a stronger light for here,' he said ruefully. 'Not very inviting at the moment, is it?'

'Of course it is — as long as you're here, Brian.' Fiona stood on tiptoe to kiss his cheek. 'You know I'd follow you anywhere.'

'That's my girl.' He smiled fondly. 'Come on, we'll just have a quick look round and get you back to Julia's. You look done in.'

Fiona gave in with a smile. 'You win! You don't fancy coming back with me? Julia did say you could stay, too, remember.'

'Don't tempt me! No, I'd better stay here and make a start on getting the place put to rights. You won't know it in the morning!'

They were just about to leave when a knocking at the door took them by surprise.

Answering it, the couple were confronted by a girl of about eighteen. Her long, wavy hair was the colour of ripe corn with the sun on it. The rest of her features combined to give her a startling, untamed beauty that wouldn't have shamed a model or a film star.

'Hello,' she said cheerily. 'I'm Shona McArthur. I believe you met my sister Eileen at the schoolhouse earlier.'

'Yes, that's right,' Brian replied. 'And don't I know your father, too — Willie McArthur?'

'That's him,' Shona replied, tossing her hair out of her eyes, as she thrust her basket towards Brian. 'Dad said to give you this.'

Puzzled, Brian looked inside. To his surprise, it contained a frisky black and white kitten.

'He's called Nicky,' Shona said.

15

'Nicky?'

'Yes. Well, Nick or Nicky, 'cause he's a wee devil. Every croft should have a good cat, Dad says.'

'He's lovely,' Fiona said, stroking the furry bundle. 'Don't you feel bad about parting with him?'

'Well, to be honest, Father wanted you to have my favourite from the litter, a wee ginger tabby. Parting with her would have been much harder.' She laughed. 'Luckily, I can twist my father around my wee finger,' she went on, 'so I've kept Ginger and you've got Nicky. Still, he should grow into a good mouser . . . '

'Mouser!'

'Yes, his mother, our cat Samantha, is a great mouser.'

'Are mice a problem around here then?' Fiona asked, not sure if Shona was teasing her.

'Well, there's the field mice in the autumn. They're cute, but they can be a problem when you get too many families of them invading your house!'

Now Fiona knew she was being teased.

'Look, Shona, come in for a few moments. We're delighted with Nicky, aren't we, Brian? Sorry about the mess in here by the way.'

'Well, since you're so delighted with your

new pet, why don't you hold him?' Brian asked, smiling.

Fiona obliged. It was strange to feel the small, warm, living creature so close to her, his tiny chest vibrating against her hand. It was almost like holding a child . . .

'And how will you like living here, Mrs Hamilton?' Shona asked, interrupting Fiona's thoughts.

'Oh — oh, I'm not sure,' she replied distractedly after a pause.

Eileen was right, Shona mused. This stranger is the quiet sort. That was all Eileen had said about her, but Shona's conclusions were much more impetuous. She decided that Fiona was rather stuck up and distant — more like *Lady* Hamilton than Mrs Hamilton.

'Well, Achnacraig suits some people,' Shona went on. 'My father thinks it's the finest place on earth. By the way,' she turned to look at Brian. 'he spoke well of you, Mr Hamilton.'

'Call me Brian, please,' he insisted. 'Well, I'm flattered to hear it.'

'Oh, ay, he minds fine when you used to come about here with your folk when you were a boy. Eileen loves Achnacraig, too. Mind you, anywhere that Duncan Campbell — he's your nearest neighbour over at Hazelbank — lives would do for Eileen. Give her Duncan and her violin playing and she'd be happy in a bothy in the middle of a peat bog.'

Brian laughed at her colourful turn of phrase.

'Is she a good fiddle player then?' he asked.

'Well, I've never heard anyone play better. She'll turn her bow to anything from 'Dark Lochnagar' to Vivaldi. She's good all right.'

'And what about you, Shona?' Fiona asked quietly. 'How do you feel about living here?'

A cold steeliness filled the girl's eyes. 'I hate it!'

★ ★ ★

Later in Julia Macpherson's cosy living-room, Fiona mentioned Shona McArthur's rather surprising attitude. Brian had gone back to Rowanlea and the two women were relaxing over a cup of coffee before they went to bed.

The friskiness of Nicky the kitten, who was tirelessly chasing a ball of wool all round the room, was a marked contrast to the exhaustion Fiona was feeling. As yet, however, she hadn't felt ready to tell Julia about her asthma.

'Yes, Shona can be a right little madam at

18

times,' Julia agreed. 'Her head's full of discos and fashions and the like — yet she's still the apple of her father's eye.'

'Really — I'd have thought Eileen . . . ' Fiona started to say.

'Now, she's the one who deserves any praise that's going!' Julia interrupted. 'She's held that family together. Eileen's the one who does all the work around the house and manages the purse. And plays the violin beautifully into the bargain.'

'Yet her father's favourite is Shona,' Fiona mused. 'It doesn't seem to add up.'

'Oh, it's simple enough, Fiona. The girl can be lazy and wayward at times, but Shona's the living image of her late mother. Willie looks at her and sees his Mary as she was when he was courting her. So Shona gets away with murder at times. This dislike of Achnacraig has been building up in her for some time now. She's grown to loathe the place almost as much as your husband loves it.'

Then Julia, ever astute, looked deep into Fiona's eyes. 'You're not as happy as Brian is about moving here, are you?'

Fiona looked up, startled. 'How did you know?' she blurted out. Then she added, 'It's what Brian wants for us — for me, really.'

'You'll grow to love this place as much as

Brian does, Fiona. You've got a wonderful husband!'

'I know. I know how lucky I am. I couldn't bear to be parted from him.'

'Cherish the time you have together.' The older woman smiled. 'Being with the man you love, sharing your life with him, is the most important thing in the world!'

They both fell silent for a few moments then Julia looked up, smiling. 'Now come on, lass, finish up your coffee and off to bed with you. Brian says he wants to set off with that van early in the morning.'

★ ★ ★

Brian Hamilton had just finished locking the doors of Rowanlea the following morning, and was thinking of heading towards the schoolhouse to say his goodbyes, when he noticed a mud-spattered pick-up heading towards him. It pulled up beside him and the driver, a dark-haired, young man whose eyes crinkled when he smiled, indicated a crate in the back.

'Good day to you. I'm Duncan Campbell from Hazelbank, the next croft up the road. I've brought some hens for you.'

The voice had the typical soft West Highland lilt.

20

'Oh, that's great. I'll stick them in the hen-house. As far as I remember, it's pretty sound.'

'Fine, I'll give you a hand,' Duncan said. 'My mother's put in a clocking hen — one that's gone broody. She'll look after the day-old chicks I hear you're to be getting. And the *cailleach's* looking out for a good cockerel for you. They're grand for keeping away the predators.'

'Here, I don't think your mother would like to hear you calling her an old woman, Duncan,' Brian remarked light-heartedly. He knew that Agnes Campbell had a reputation for being a pretty forceful character.

'Och, she'd like it fine. She knows cailleach's just a term of endearment.'

The two men chuckled companionably. Then, their work done, Brian excused himself, explaining he had a long drive ahead of him.

This unexpected hold-up meant he was running behind schedule when he reached the schoolhouse and he had to cut his goodbyes to Fiona shorter than he meant to.

'Cheer up,' he said with a smile, noticing his wife's disappointment. 'I'll be back before you know it, and I'll have our own car. That'll make quite a difference to us here.'

'Well, take care, darling,' she said, reaching up to kiss him.

'You, too, love,' he murmured.

Julia Macpherson had discreetly left them on their own, but when she heard the van pulling away she went back into the sitting-room to join Fiona.

'Is that him safely on his way then?' she asked brightly.

'Yes,' the girl replied. 'And I'm missing him already.'

'Och well, he won't be gone long, Fiona. Do you fancy another cup of tea to cheer us up meantime? You're looking a bit pale.'

Fiona smiled at her attentive hostess. There was no doubt she'd found a friend in Julia Macpherson.

'Yes, I'd love a cuppa. But, look, I'll make it this time. You've done enough.'

She was about to stand up when Julia stopped her.

'No — no,' she said. 'You save your strength for Rowanlea. You'll need it.'

In the kitchen she busied herself making the tea and preparing a tray of home-baked scones. As a finishing touch, she put some of Agnes Campbell's delicious blackberry jam into a dainty dish. Satisfied with the effect, she carried it all through to the sitting-room.

To her concern, Fiona was looking paler than ever. 'Are you all right, dear?'

'Well, to be honest, I'm not feeling too great,' Fiona gasped.

As her guest's breathing became more laboured, Julia's anxiety mounted. Before her eyes, Fiona began to gasp for air.

One thing was patently obvious to Julia — Fiona desperately needed help. So after sitting the girl in an armchair and handing her the handbag she had frantically signalled for, Julia dashed out to the hall to telephone Ian Frazer, the local GP. It seemed an age before his receptionist answered the phone and even longer before Ian's deep voice sounded in her ear.

'This had better be important, Julia,' he started crustily.

However, as the urgency of Julia's words got through to him, the doctor's attitude changed.

'Fiona Hamilton, you say? Yes, I've had a letter about her from a specialist in Glasgow. Look, Julia, the girl's asthmatic. Make sure she uses the inhaler she's been prescribed — quickly! I'm on my way now.'

Slamming the phone down, Julia was about to go back to Fiona when a sudden thought struck her. Shouldn't Brian Hamilton be with his wife at this time? But how could she contact him? Quickly she realised there was a way . . .

Without further delay, she lifted the receiver and dialled Willie McArthur's number.

* * *

'Hello,' the man's gentle, lilting voice replied.

'Willie? Julia Macpherson here. I need a favour — quickly.'

'Of course, what is it?'

'Look, could you get in your car and catch Brian Hamilton? He's not long away from here and he's in that hired van, so he shouldn't be too far up the shore road.'

'Fair enough, but what's the problem?'

'It's his wife. She's been taken ill. Look, I can't go into too much detail. Just tell him it's not too serious.'

'OK, Julia — I'm on my way.'

Putting down the receiver again, Julia hurried through to see how Fiona was faring. To her intense relief, the girl seemed much more in control, having had the presence of mind to fish out her inhaler from her handbag.

'Are you feeling a bit better, dear?' she asked anxiously.

'Yes, just a bit washed out. These attacks always take a lot out of me. Look, Julia, I'm sorry to have upset you like this. It must have been a shock for you.' Fiona was still breathing heavily.

'Well, I must admit it was a bit scary. I just wish you'd told me about your asthma.'

'I — I know I should have, but I didn't want to burden you with my troubles.'

'That was silly, dear. Anyway, it's all water under the bridge now and Dr Frazer's on his way. Is there anything I can do for you in the meantime?'

'No,' Fiona said wearily, 'you've done more than enough already. Well, not unless you can fetch Brian back for me,' she added jokingly.

'Oh, don't worry about that. It's already in hand.'

'I don't know how to thank you, Julia,' Fiona began, 'you seem to have thought of everything.'

'Well, just you think about getting better.'

'Now that's what I call good advice!' Dr Ian Frazer's voice startled both women. 'I just let myself in, Julia.'

'Fiona, this is Dr Frazer.'

Looking at this slim, middle-aged man with the mop of iron-grey hair, Fiona instinctively felt she would be in good hands.

'Now, how are you doing, young lady?'

'Tired, doctor, but bearing up.'

'Ay, you'll be worn out right enough.'

Dr Fraser was very much the old-fashioned caring family doctor, but he didn't mince his words when it came to offering guidance.

'Asthma can be a frightening condition,' he went on, 'but its treatment now is a lot more effective than it was in my early days. We used to say that the medicines we prescribed were worse than the illness, Fiona.'

He smiled down at her.

'All the same, it's important that you fight it and learn to stand on your own two feet. You're a sensible girl — that's obvious from the way you used your inhaler when you needed to. So don't let that husband of yours mollycoddle you. He'll want to at times, but just you let him see that you're far from being an invalid.'

'I'll do my best, Dr Frazer,' Fiona promised.

'Good girl! Well now, I've had a letter from your specialist, so we'll just follow his advice — as long as I agree with what he says,' he added with a twinkle in his eye.

Just then the door opened slightly and Nicky, the kitten, who'd been snoozing in the cupboard under Julia's stair, came in.

Dr Frazer's jaw dropped. 'Julia, get that cat out of here!' he ordered. 'I'll lay ten to one that he's the cause of this latest attack.'

He turned to Fiona. 'Have you ever had a kitten before?'

'No, never.'

'Well, I'll bet you're allergic to cats. That could be enough to trigger off a bronchial spasm. Of course, we'd need to do the tests to be really sure, but my instincts are seldom wrong. Now, my girl, if you're feeling a bit better, I think we'll get you into bed. I'll have to check you over and think about prescribing some drugs that'll help.'

'What about your house calls, Ian?' Julia interrupted.

'Och, there's nothing too urgent. I might have to phone a couple of patients, if you don't mind. But perhaps you could rustle up a pot of tea while I chat to Fiona. No, I'm in no hurry.'

★ ★ ★

Away from the restored calm of the schoolhouse, Willie McArthur was hurtling along the shore road at unaccustomed speed. Luckily, he knew every twist and turn of the winding route and he was actually warming to his urgent task. Even so, it took him quite a while to catch up with Brian Hamilton's blue van.

'Sorry to startle you like that, Brian, but

27

I've been sent to fetch you back.'

'Go back — what on earth for?'

'Julia says it's nothing too serious, but your wife's been taken poorly.'

Guessing what the problem was, Brian didn't waste time asking questions.

'Right then, Willie. Let's get back.'

'Well, mind and take it easy. These roads can be really treacherous at times.'

When they reached the schoolhouse, Willie McArthur took his leave to prepare for the night's fishing, and Brian rushed in to see Fiona.

Dr Frazer, who'd been with his patient all the time, intercepted him in the hallway.

'Take it easy, Mr Hamilton,' he told the distraught-looking man. 'Your wife is fast asleep. You can look in on her by all means, but I think our best course is to let her be. Sleep's the best medicine for Fiona just now. Oh, I'm Dr Frazer, by the way.' They shook hands briefly. 'Off you go then, but don't wake her or you'll have me to answer to.'

Brian tiptoed into the darkened bedroom and looked down on his wife's lovely features. She looked so pale and exhausted. His normally exuberant spirits plummeted, even as his heart filled with love for his young wife.

After a few moments he left the bedroom

28

and went back to join Julia and the doctor in the kitchen.

'All right now?' Ian Frazer asked him.

'No, no it's far from all right,' he said, distressed. 'I can't help feeling that bringing Fiona here was the biggest mistake I've made in my life!'

A Spectacular Storm

Nonsense!' Dr Frazer dismissed Brian's feelings of guilt. 'What did Mr Evans say when you told him you were coming here?'

'He was delighted. That's when he said he'd write to you . . . ' Brian sighed heavily. 'But — we're only just here, and Fiona's had two attacks already. One on the way and another one now . . . '

'The first attack,' said the doctor deliberately, 'was brought on by the effort and excitement of moving. The second — by the kitten.'

'The kitten?' Brian repeated.

'Yes. It's a common allergy. I'm pretty certain it's to blame in this case.'

'So . . . it could have happened anywhere?' Brian regarded him hopefully.

'Anywhere,' the doctor assured him.

'Well . . . ' Relief flooded Brian's face. The hollow feeling inside him began to disappear. 'What should I do, then?'

'Nothing. You might as well take the van back . . . '

'Your coffee will be cold,' Julia told Brian, coming in from the scullery with a fresh brew.

'Good heavens!' He looked at his watch. 'The morning's gone! I'll never get the van back and be able to return before nightfall.'

'Have you anyone you can stay with in Glasgow?' Julia asked.

'Well, there's a slight problem there. My mother stays with my married sister and her youngsters, but they're all on holiday just now. Still, I'm sure I could find a friend to put me up. If I could use your phone . . . '

'Go ahead,' said Julia. 'What about phoning Duncan Campbell, too, and asking him to feed those hens he brought you? Or do you want me to go up?'

'Heavens, no! We've been enough trouble to you. And on a Saturday, too. Your day off!'

'I wish I could have a day off!' Dr Frazer complained. 'There's a trout I'm after . . . '

Julia smiled as she began to show the two men out.

Brian hesitated for a moment. 'Do you think I should wake Fiona to say goodbye?' he asked.

'No, don't,' the doctor replied emphatically. 'I've given her an injection to help her sleep.'

Brian nodded. 'In that case, Julia, will you explain, and tell her I'll phone before the day's out?'

'Of course, Brian.'

'And I'll come round in the evening, Julia.' Dr Frazer lifted his case. 'I'm going to get my rods out this afternoon, I hope.' His last words were drowned in a loud roar from a souped-up exhaust system, shattering the silence of the village.

'It's a blessing the patient's in a back room,' Ian Frazer snapped angrily.

'So much for the peace and quiet of Achnacraig!' Brian laughed. 'What on earth was that?'

'The local land-owner had a rally for customised, highly-tuned cars last weekend. That's his own hobby.' Julia had opened the door but she pushed it shut again.

'From all accounts he'd a splendid route mapped out over some of his forest land,' put in the doctor. 'Fortunately, all the other cars have gone!'

'Only this one remains.' Julia peered out to where she could still see it. 'And that's because it belongs to Shona McArthur's new boyfriend, who's lingered on . . .'

'Bloomin' nuisance of a thing it is, too!' grumbled the doctor with a brief wave before moving off towards his car.

★ ★ ★

Three houses along, Willie McArthur's thoughts echoed the doctor's.

After its loud, roaring approach, the car had braked with a nerve-shearing growl outside his gate.

A few moments before, Willie had poured himself a well-earned dram, after his mercy dash for Brian Hamilton. Could a fellow not have a bit of peace in his own house? All he wanted was to relax for a bit before getting down to his boat.

He sat down in his chair, but his body remained tense. His daughter would be sitting out there making a spectacle of herself with that strange young man, and the whole village looking on from behind their curtains!

When Shona flounced in, looking as if she didn't care about anyone or anything, that did it.

His temper snapped. 'Nice of you to spare your family a little of your time for a change!' Willie's Highland voice was icy.

There was a defiant glint in Shona's eyes. Her cheeks were flushed and her lovely hair streamed everywhere.

'Could you not tell that lad of yours to tone down that dreadful machine? It's driving the whole village mad! And, not only that, there's a sick woman in the schoolhouse!'

'Huh!' Shona tossed her head. 'That'll be

33

Lady Hamilton, no doubt. Julia's never ill!'

'Ach, have you no sympathy? Shona, Shona — what kind of a lass are you turning out to be?' Willie caught his breath. He didn't know how to handle this for the best. If only their mother hadn't been taken when the girls were so young . . .

'It's not just me.' Willie rubbed a hand over his eyes. 'The folk in the village keep mentioning that roaring dragon to me. They want none of it here!'

Shona hurled her shoulder-bag with venom into a chair.

'That's just what's wrong with this place!' she yelled, rage flaring in her blue eyes. 'Bring a little colour and excitement in — and everyone complains! They're all dead here! They're boring — and they're dead, dead!' Her voice echoed round the room. She stalked to the lobby door. 'Thank goodness there's a disco at Portmelford tonight!'

'But that's six miles away,' he called after her. 'You mind how you go. That car might be built for speed, but these roads aren't — I can tell you!'

Shona put her head back round the door. 'I don't want to be told any more!' She spat the words, slammed the door, and rushed upstairs to her room.

Willie looked helplessly at the closed door

then tossed back the whole dram that he'd meant to sip and enjoy.

In the kitchen, Eileen set a tray and started to re-heat the soup she'd made that morning. A born homemaker, she dealt with each crisis with calm practicality. She wondered if she should take some soup up to Shona.

Shona could be maddening. Eileen wished she would help her more. She was for ever covering up for her so that their father wouldn't realise how often Shona shirked the few tasks she was asked to do.

But, Eileen thought as she checked the rolls she'd put to heat, Shona had been only ten when their mother had died. Perhaps both she and her father had tried too hard to make up to her for the loss. Eileen, two years older, had swiftly taken over the running of the home in addition to her schoolwork. At the time the extra workload had in fact helped her through her grief.

Shona was artistic. Now eighteen, she helped a hairdresser who came to the hotel twice a week but she hadn't decided yet if she'd make that her career.

Her father, Eileen felt, didn't care if Shona did nothing, just as long as she stayed with him. But her sister realised that she was discontented and restless, in need of more employment.

'Shona should help more in the house,' Willie said as he took his soup from Eileen.

'It's OK, Dad, honestly. I feel keeping the house running smoothly is my job.'

'Everything's fallen on your shoulders, Eileen. I should have been more firm with Shona,' Willie said regretfully.

'Maybe we've both spoiled her, Dad.'

'Ay. Maybe we have. And where has it all led? Maybe now I'm retiring I'll have more time to keep an eye on her.'

Eileen laughed ruefully. 'Dad, I don't think a girl of that age would fancy having an eye kept on her!'

When Willie had finished his soup, he stood up and announced that he was away down to the boat to check a few things before the night's fishing.

Eileen was relieved. When he'd gone, she quickly gathered up the crockery. She had a meeting that afternoon and she didn't want her father to know about it.

★ ★ ★

Help yourself to some lunch, Shona,' Eileen called up to her sister, as she let herself out of the house. Carrying her violincase with her, she walked along to the village hall. This was to be the venue for her father's retiral party, which he wasn't supposed to know about yet.

Willie was due to retire from the sea, both as skipper of his fishing boat and from the local lifeboat. Everyone in the village agreed that such an important occasion couldn't go unrecognised. A committee had been set up to consider how best to celebrate the event, and a special ceilidh decided on.

Eileen and Duncan Campbell led the committee, ably supported by Julia Macpherson and Andrew Neilson. The latter owned the boatyard and had the job of being the representative of the local seaman's mission. A number of the local ladies, including Duncan's mother, had been co-opted for the catering and refreshments for the evening.

Duncan and Eileen's first task was to consider the programme. This had to be done early as it involved approaching singers and musicians, not only locally, but also from the surrounding area.

★ ★ ★

When Eileen reached the hall, she found that the door was open. Duncan was up on the platform tinkering with the piano keys, and he turned round as she entered.

She walked towards him in the empty hall,

her pulse accelerating as it always did when she saw him.

'Come up beside me,' he said, leaning down and taking her hand to pull her up the three steps. She laughed as she joined him, and swung away, stifling the nervousness that took hold of her when she was near him, and went to place her violin on top of the piano.

'Well,' Duncan said, propping himself on the piano stool, 'where do we start?'

'I thought,' Eileen pulled the chair Duncan had set for her a little further away from him. 'I thought we'd arrange the tables at the back of the hall. And — what do you think of this, Duncan — ' she demonstrated with her hands ' — a sort of trellis coming out a bit on both sides, screening off the buffet area?'

'Great!'

'But how could we do it?' she asked.

'Leave it to Andrew. If a boat-builder can't contrive that . . . And you could put some plants or greenery along the bottom.'

'That's what I thought!' Eileen said enthusiastically.

'Two minds! I always knew we'd make a great team, Eileen.'

Colour ran up into her cheeks as they went on to discuss the programme of entertainment.

'Maybe some games, and lots of dances,' she said breathlessly, 'like 'Strip The Willow' and 'The Dashing White Sergeant', to warm them all up. Then later, the musical items, in between dances. Oh, and we must have songs with choruses everyone can join in!'

'We'll soon arrange that,' Duncan told her confidently.

'Will you get the ceilidh band together — yourself and the others?'

'Sure. But I don't want to be fiddling all night. I want to dance with you.' Duncan smiled.

'Well, I'll be busy, too, helping with the food and so on.' Eileen looked down quickly.

'Och, ay. And it's your father's do after all — not our wedding!'

'Duncan! Will you stop teasing — and concentrate!' Eileen said with exasperation.

'You'll be giving us a tune on the night?' he asked.

'I thought I'd play some of Dad's favourites.'

'Hey! I've just remembered! What are you doing here? Why aren't you away to Fort William for your violin lesson today?' Duncan suddenly demanded.

'I've had my last one. Mrs Morrison says there's nothing more she can do for me.

From here on, I need a really professional tutor.'

Duncan gave her a long look of dismay. 'No! What will you do? Is there anyone else?'

'I doubt it. I doubt there'll not be another concert violinist coming to these parts — just because I need a new teacher!' Her shoulders slumped suddenly and her eyes became shadowed by a haunting sadness.

'But, you can't just let it go! Let your skill just — rust!'

'That's what Mrs Morrison said, too. She wants me to keep practising — hours and hours each day. She says I've got a rare talent.'

'That's why she took you on when you were just a wee lassie at school!'

'Yes.'

Duncan couldn't stand to see her looking so downcast. 'Come on!' He rallied. 'Tell me what you're going to play for us at the ceilidh!'

Eileen jerked up. 'Och, even if I told you, you'd be none the wiser!' she teased him, a smile finding the corners of her mouth.

He grinned back. 'Come on!' He stood up. 'You have your violin, so play! Please?'

He set up her music stand then settled into a chair behind Eileen, waiting for the music to begin. A shaft of sunlight came through a side window like a searchlight and touched Eileen's smooth head as she tuned up the violin. Then the soft pure notes were pouring into the hall.

She played a piece that he didn't recognise, but in two minutes there were tears in his eyes. She made the violin say things that words couldn't convey. She made it yearn and sob. It was almost beyond bearing when the piece at last came to an end in a final, agonised whisper.

Dunan had only time to take in a deep breath and move stiff limbs, when Eileen swung into an old Gaelic air. The violin was now laughing and comforting and crooning to him.

He felt exhausted, as though he'd been on an emotional see-saw. What kind of a talent was it that Eileen possessed? It was so much a part of her that you couldn't consider Eileen without her music.

She had received a gift. The thought stabbed him. *A talent must not be wasted!* But that talent would be the thing that would almost certainly transport her out of his life for ever.

★ ★ ★

Shona was heady with excitement. The loud, throbbing music and the brilliant, flashing lights seemed to have possessed her, and she was dancing with frenzied energy. This was living, she thought rapturously, this was life. It was so effortless. Her body responded to the music and carried her away. She'd never felt so elated in her life. She seemed to be not just in another village, but on another planet.

Tony Wilkinson was impressed with her. He could see there was rhythm in her soul. She was like a wild wave, indefatigable — and she was immensely attractive. He knew a number of pretty girls at college but when, the week before, Shona had walked into the dance at Achnacraig, he'd been unable to take his eyes off her, and had monopolised her for the entire evening.

The pounding music came to a temporary halt and he was able to make himself heard.

'Let's go for a drink. I'm thirsty.'

'But this is marvellous!' Shona's eyes sparkled. 'I don't want to stop. I don't need anything.'

'You're going to stop, 'cos we both need something to drink!' He caught her hand and, laughing, pulled her towards the partition, behind which lay the refreshment area. There he settled them at a small table with long glasses of fresh orange juice and ice.

The music started again and, even there, they had to shout to make themselves heard.

'It's great. I love it!' Shona declared. 'I've never been to such a super disco! What a difference from boring old Achnacraig. Oh, how I hate that place!'

'I don't know why you stick it then.' Tony was matter-of-fact. He put his glass down and placed his elbow over the back of his chair.

He was a good-looking young man with light-brown hair, worn rather long — giving him a rakish look that delighted Shona.

'I've no choice.' Moodily she rattled the ice cubes around her glass.

'That's nonsense! You're old enough to be independent. We could be enjoying bright lights and great sounds every night in Glasgow.'

Lifting her head, she stared incredulously at him for a moment, excitement beginning to grow in her.

Tony nodded confidently, his warm gaze devouring her.

'Yes. There are discos there that make this place look like a kid's party!'

'Oh, I'd love to see a proper light show!' Shona's voice was full of longing.

'Well, that would be easy enough to arrange. It's a shame I have to get back tomorrow. I shouldn't have stayed as long as I have. I must get through that exam this time.'

'Yes.' Shona tried to hide the feeling of utter desolation that suddenly swept over her at his words. She'd been living on an ecstatic cloud nine since they'd met a week ago. When the other rally members had left, Tony had stayed, and they'd been in each other's company constantly.

'This is our last night together. We'll have to make the most of it.' She swallowed. 'Goodness only knows how I'll manage without you. I wish I could come with you.'

He leaned across the table and took both her hands in his.

'That wouldn't be sensible, Shona. I really have to study for that exam.' He searched her face intently.

'All the same,' he went on casually, 'I know a lot of girls sharing flats. If you're serious about leaving here, I could probably put out a few feelers. I should think, especially at the end of term, we could get you fixed up with somewhere to stay.'

'Really, Tony?' Shona's eyes suddenly shone like stars.

He let go of her hands, his gaze sweeping over her. The blue shade of her dress was just right for her eyes, her blonde hair had a ruffled softness about it, and there was an air of recklessness about her that seemed to make her glow. She was magic.

'Sure,' he said with resolution. 'If that's what you want. I'll drop you a line when I've sussed something out.'

'Promise?' she asked wistfully, not sure of him now, sensing that the student life would soon take him over again.

'I promise,' he assured her.

'Well, if you find somewhere for me to stay, I'll be out of here like a rocket. As soon as I hear from you — I'll get the bus — and to blazes with the lot of them!'

★ ★ ★

It was late the following morning when Brian turned his small hatchback down the loch-side road towards Achnacraig. When he'd first sighted the loch, a slight wind was ruffling the surface of the water. Now, as he drove on, he saw a tell-tale roll of black cloud, which he knew might herald a squall, coming up over the sound. Two anglers, out in a rowing boat, looked up, read the signs, and quickly made for the shore.

45

Those spectacular Highland storms could finish as quickly as they started, and the gale sweep off into the mountains. The crofter-fishermen knew, from long experience, just when one was likely to strike and, given these extra minutes, would make for shelter. As Brian's mind ran on these thoughts, a sudden blast of wind, laden with sleety rain, hit his windscreen, sluicing thickly down the glass. Hastily he switched on the wipers and eased his foot off the accelerator. It would be good to get home.

He was longing to be with Fiona again and to see for himself just how well she was recovering. Julia had reassured him when they'd spoken on the phone the night before.

Visibility had become very poor. Brian had to slow down again and switch on the lights as he negotiated the narrow road. Peering through the sheets of rain, he caught sight of a solitary, rain-soaked figure, standing by a farm-gate, and wildly flagging him down.

He brought the car to a sudden halt in a flurry of surface water, and the stranger wrenched open the passenger door.

'Quick! Can you take me to the harbour?'

'Sure — jump in!'

The man had such an air of urgency about him that, almost before he'd got in, Brian had accelerated off again.

'McRory's my name. I'm a member of the lifeboat crew — and we've just had a call-out!'

'I'll drive as quickly as I can!' Brian assured him.

'Don't take any chances!' The young man rubbed his hand down a narrow, ruddy face to remove the water. His copper hair was flattened and darkened by the rain.

'I should have been there by now,' he said in a harassed voice.

'How do they get in touch with you?'

'We've all got bleepers now. But they set the maroons off as well. I was getting some animals in before the squall would strike. And then, when I got to the car, I found I'd a flat tyre!'

'Bad luck!' Brian put on a little more speed. 'But, don't worry, we won't be long now. I wonder what's happened.'

Fiona Hamilton and Julia Macpherson had also become very aware of the driving wind. In no time at all it had increased in strength and was volleying and buffeting round the strong school-house walls.

'It can blow up in an instant,' Julia told Fiona, joining her at the window, 'and just as quickly blow over again.'

'Look how the waves are being whipped

up! It's quite spectacular!' Fiona was excitedly watching the show nature was putting on.

'You're looking much better this morning, Fiona. I'm so glad.'

'I'm feeling a lot better, Julia, thank you. Oh, look!' She rose on her toes as she watched the gyrations of the massing, white-topped breakers. 'Isn't that something out there? I can hardly see through the rain and the sea keeps changing.'

'Mmm.' Julia searched for her binoculars. 'It's a small motor-launch,' she said, focusing the glasses. 'It looks to me as though it's been making for the harbour and has lost power.'

She handed the binoculars to Fiona. 'That must have been the reason for the maroons going off for the lifeboat. Willie McArthur and his boys will soon sort everything out.'

'Oh, I hope so,' Fiona said quietly. 'You have to admire the courage of men who go out in conditions like that.'

Through the binoculars, Fiona watched the small boat lifting and plunging in the heavy seas, gradually being swept towards the rocky outcrop on the other shore of the bay.

'I hope the lifeboat gets a move on. There are some nasty currents out there,' Julia observed. She found herself unwilling to take her eyes off the helpless boat, as if

48

by watching over her she could keep her safe till the lifeboatmen got there.

'The sea's frightening at times,' Fiona was still sharing Julia's vigil. 'I'm glad Brian's on shore for good now. I wonder how he's getting on driving back in this?'

At last they spotted the lifeboat coming from the harbour and relief flooded over them. Then they heard a knock on the inner door and swung round as Eileen McArthur came into the room.

'What a day!' She gasped. 'Sorry to butt in like this, but I've got a message for you.' She threw back the hood of her streaming raincoat and wiped strands of wet hair back from her face.

'Actually it's for Fiona.' Eileen was still breathless with hurrying, aware of the two pairs of eyes riveted on her. And Fiona felt a stab of uneasiness go through her.

'I've to tell you that Brian won't be back till the lifeboat comes in again.'

Fiona's uneasiness became an icy coldness somewhere in the pit of her stomach.

'He's gone out with them,' Eileen went on. 'He says to tell you he'll explain it all when he gets home.'

The Call Of The Sea

In a little over an hour, the lifeboat was back at her station. Julia, Fiona and Eileen peered anxiously through the rain and spray, and with the help of Julia's binoculars had actually seen her take the motor-launch in tow.

When the two boats had finally disappeared round the sheltering arm of the harbour wall, the three watchers sighed with relief.

Julia went off to make some coffee, and had just begun pouring it out when they heard the sounds of the men returning.

Fiona ran out into the hall and was caught up in Brian's arms. Love and relief flooded over her and she clung to him, oblivious of everything else.

'How are you, love?' Brian's voice sounded husky. 'I wanted to get back to you as quickly as possible. And would have . . . but for this hold-up!'

'I'm fine, now. Honestly!' she murmured.

'Sure?' he asked, gazing into her eyes with concern.

'Sure!' She smiled. 'Now you're back.'

Brian kissed her, set her down and turned,

with his arm still round her, to the older man standing behind him.

'This is Willie McArthur, Fiona. He's been looking forward to meeting you.'

'How do you do, Mr McArthur? Now I've met all the family!'

Fiona's happiness made her glow, and they shook hands warmly.

The two men followed Fiona into Julia's living-room, and were soon supplied with steaming mugs of coffee.

'Well, and how are you now, Mistress Hamilton?' Willie settled back in his chair, warming his hands on his beaker. 'I've come to find out. I've been worrying about you ever since I dashed up the shore road to turn Brian back!'

'It was good of you, Mr McArthur. I'm feeling much stronger now. Thank you. And do call me Fiona.'

'I was sorry to snatch your husband away again, there, when he was hurrying back to you . . . But, oh, my, he was a grand help to us — and just when we needed him!'

'What went wrong, Willie?' Julie asked.

'Well, as usual, haste was important. And, before Brian and Rory arrived at the station, we were still two men short. We'd no radio man. As the coxswain, even with Rory there, I'd to decide whether to go off a man short.

'Well, Brian volunteered to stand in because it was an emergency, and he was a great asset. It was as if he'd always been one of the team, and his experience with the communications was invaluable. I'm deeply grateful to you, lad!'

'It was nothing.' Brian shrugged his shoulders.

Willie put down his mug. 'Let me be the judge of that,' he said quietly. 'The other thing I came round for,' he added heartily, 'was to ask you and Fiona to come to my retirement party.'

Brian's face lit up. 'Thank you very much, Willie. We'd love to come. Wouldn't we, Fiona?'

'Oh, yes. We would indeed!'

Eileen looked at Julia ruefully. 'He found out,' she said lamely.

'I had a feeling he might!' Julia laughed.

'Well.' Willie rose to his feet, his smile widening to a grin. 'That's settled then. It'll be a chance for you to meet a lot more of the people from hereabouts.'

'It's very kind of you,' Brian began.

'Havers! We were glad of you today.'

'Weren't you scared, Brian?' Fiona turned to her husband, smiling, happiness and relief still surging in her heart.

'Scared? No! We didn't have time to be!' He got up to join Willie and stood looking down at his wife, his eyes glowing. 'In all honesty, Fiona, I can say I loved every minute of it. I hadn't realised just how much I'd been missing the sea!'

Fiona looked taken aback by the sheer passion of Brian's reply. In the silence that followed it, hot colour ran up into the delicate skin of her cheeks, and her lids dropped swiftly to cover eyes that had darkened with doubt.

Julia looked at her in silent compassion, and then at Eileen, alert and thoughtful, studying her father's face.

Willie had turned his head sharply and was staring steadily and shrewdly at Brian. Eileen had seen that look before. It wasn't so much a sailor's look — more the look of a fisherman about to hook something!

★ ★ ★

The croft living-room at Rowanlea was beginning to look like home, although some tea-chests stood about still waiting to be unpacked. A bright fire crackled in the hearth.

Fiona had inspected the whole place in the daylight. The cottage had been extended to form a bathroom, opening off the central passageway, and a new, beautifully-fitted kitchen added on behind the living-room.

The kitchen was well provided with cupboards and there was also an electric cooker, and a small fridge. The back door opened on to a yard surrounded by out-buildings in various stages of disrepair.

'There seems a lot to be done,' Fiona remarked hesitantly when Brian followed her to the door.

'Yes, there is but we'll get through it all, don't worry,' he assured her. 'But first I must make the brooder for the chicks I brought back with me. I'm away to get started.' And so saying, he made his way to the nearest shed.

Fiona went indoors and started unpacking dishes and cooking utensils. After she'd been busy for a while, she found herself being drawn to have another peep at the chicks. She knew she risked another asthma attack, but she felt herself tugged towards them. She lifted out one that looked too delicate to live. Its eyes were closed. She felt her throat tighten in sympathy.

Inside her began to coil the same helpless longing that she'd felt holding the tiny kitten. Was it only because the doctor had warned her against having children yet, that this awful feeling of frustration was gnawing at her?

She placed the scrap of life back in the centre of the box, affording it maximum warmth and support from its fellows, and rose resolutely to her feet. There was work to be done.

★ ★ ★

It was evening before they'd finished unpacking and had most of their possessions in place. And it wasn't until after nine o'clock when, tired but satisfied, they sat down to a meal.

'Crikey, this is impressive, Fiona!' Brian congratulated her. 'How on earth did you manage spaghetti bolognese? Smells terrific!'

'Must you know all my secrets? I made it with a tin of mince. Where are you going?'

'You just reminded me. Wait a minute. There's something in the car that Marion and Bob gave me . . . '

He returned shortly, carrying a bottle of wine.

'It's to handsel the house, they said.'

'That was nice of them! How were they, by the way? I forgot to ask.' Fiona smiled at the thought of her old friends.

'Fine. They're coming up to see us when we get settled.'

'That'll be great — I'm sure we'll have a lot of visitors. Your mum will have to come and we'll have to ask my aunt and uncle, too, sometime.'

What was intended as a scratch meal turned out to be a celebratory feast. After their exertions, the food and wine tasted especially good. Warm and relaxed, curled up in the easy chair with her coffee, Fiona suddenly remembered the small cat.

'Will the kitten be all right in the shed?'

'Snug as a bug in a rug, and so will you be in a minute. Come on, off to bed the moment you've finished your coffee.'

'Dr Frazer said I was to be sturdy and independent, and not let you coddle me.'

'Well, Dr Hamilton's tidying up. You go on. I won't be long.'

When Brian came upstairs, Fiona was lying in bed admiring the effect he'd achieved in the room. The blue carpeting looked rich against the white walls and paintwork, which shone softly in the glow from the bed lamps. It was their first night at Rowanlea, but already she was experiencing a feeling of homecoming.

Brian had the tidy habits of a sailor. She enjoyed watching him quickly taking off his clothes, then, in contrast, very neatly folding them and putting them away.

How handsome he was! The lamplight shone on his well-built body, which never seemed to lose its healthy tan. His arms were the colour of bronze; his hands, broad and practical, dusted with fine gold hairs. He had a look of strength and endurance.

What beautiful children he could have had — if only he'd had a different wife!

'I like to watch you,' she whispered, her voice full of tenderness. His hair, still wet from his shower, lay in damp tendrils on his forehead and neck.

She was losing herself in the vision of his strong, masculine form. He was a man who loved action: loved the sea. More than he loved her? She pushed the thought aside as childish and unworthy.

He turned from his careful folding and saw her eyes devouring him and, neither moving, they regarded each other for a long moment. She saw his eyes darken with passion as they studied her with an intensity that thrilled her. Her body became warm with excitement, and suddenly she was in his arms.

★ ★ ★

The village hall was alive with music and laughter. Willie McArthur's retiral party was in full flood. The ceilidh band was excelling

57

itself. Fiddle, accordion, drums and piano played strenuous and beguiling airs that had everyone dancing or tapping their feet.

'I like the way the programme's arranged so that every dance is interspersed with a musical item,' Fiona said as she flopped down beside Brian after a lively military two-step.

'Gives you a chance to have a rest!' Brian agreed, mopping his brow.

'Even the children know every step of 'Strip The Willow' and the eightsome reels and things. They're amazing. Where do folk get all the energy from?'

'It's the music.' A man standing beside them joined in the conversation. 'When the music starts we can't help but dance!' He laughed and sat down on the empty seat beside Fiona.

Brian leaned forward. 'Fiona, this is Andrew Neilson — of the Seamen's Mission. My wife, Fiona, Andrew.'

Fiona smiled, then the company was hushed as the next item was announced — a song from Julia Macpherson.

After the encore, the strains of 'Coming Through The Rye,' in an easy waltz time, were soon coaxing the dancers back on the floor.

★ ★ ★

Fiona found herself looking up into kind eyes that contained a lurking humour and looked as though, at any moment, they might crinkle into laughter.

'What is the mission work you do?' she asked Andrew.

'It's an institution that helps widows and orphans of fishermen — or injured fishermen. It was set up by a James Wilson, an Achnacraig man, who amassed a fortune in the textile industry. He founded it in memory of his father who was tragically lost at sea.'

'Do you enjoy the work?'

'It's satisfying.' He swung her expertly to avoid a collision with Brian and Shona, who were also on the floor. 'As well as being able to provide financial aid through the mission, I can often offer comfort and advice . . . ' He gave a self-deprecating smile.

'You won't . . . Well, hopefully, you won't be doing that all the time?' Fiona enquired.

'No. I have a boatyard. We're busy there, mostly with repairs, all the year round.' He looked down with more interest at the girl he was dancing with. There was a rather frail look about her. Good thing she had a strong husband in Brian to shoulder the knocks of life for her.

When they were leaving the floor they were joined by Shona and Brian.

'Let's find seats,' Shona coaxed. 'Eileen's going to play for Dad now.'

Eileen stood alone on the platform and a hush descended on the hall. Then, from the moment the first pure notes winged out from the violin, the audience was enraptured. It was as though Eileen had discovered the rare ability to draw out the deepest secrets of the heart, hauntingly, from the violin.

Soft sighs escaped from many throats as the selection of Willie's favourite pieces drew to a close. Then the violin became a fiddle, and out leaped a bright jig to set feet tapping again.

A great cheer and tumultuous clapping followed Eileen from the platform and continued as she made her way up the hall.

'She was inspired tonight!' whispered an old Highland woman, Rhona Morrison, to Julia Macpherson.

'She played like an angel,' Julia stated, unashamedly wiping away a tear. 'You started something, Rhona, when you taught her as a wee lassie.'

'Just the rudiments, Julia. Just the rudiments.

She's gone far beyond me now. But she really is special. And we can't have that gift wasted. I've an idea, Julia . . . But here she comes!'

Eileen, reaching them, gave each a warm smile.

'Congratulations, Eileen,' Rhona Morrison said. 'That was just beautiful.'

'Well, it was you who started me off the right way, Mrs Morrison.'

'No, you've a gift there, lass. That kind of talent was gifted by God, not me!'

All three laughed at the old lady's vehemence. But she became serious again.

'It would be wrong not to develop your talent further, Eileen,' she insisted. 'I know I sound like an old nag. I'm always telling you this, and so is Julia.'

'I know, I know,' Eileen interrupted gently. 'But what more can I do? I practise. I do all the exercises . . . But, you say you can't teach me any more and there's nobody else . . . '

'Ah.' Mrs Morrison shot a triumphant glance at Julia. 'Listen to this. I know folk who could teach you a lot more yet, Eileen. I was just about to tell Julia. I've been in contact with a very great violin teacher I know. I knew him as a boy. His aunt lived near me and we were very friendly.

'Anyway, he's running a series of auditions in a few weeks' time. If you pass — and the standards are very high — you could end up being offered a full-time course. It would mean you travelling to London.'

'You mean I could go!' Eileen gasped.

'Well, nothing's been finalised. He doesn't take on just anyone, you know. And I had to sound you out first. But, frankly, it's a marvellous opportunity, and all I have to do is pull a few strings as far as the audition is concerned. The rest would be up to you. You think about what I've said and let me know within a week. It's an intensive, three-year course for specially-talented violinists.'

A sudden surge of ambition rose in Eileen. The thought of furthering her musical ability — the one thing in her life that most fulfilled her — glittered and beckoned. Her eyes sparkled, she looked back to the platform where she'd stood a few moments before, glorying in her gift of bringing pleasure to her father and their friends.

Then she saw Duncan walk on to the stage and pick up his fiddle. Her heart lurched. Duncan! How could she live without seeing him for all that time?

★ ★ ★

Willie McArthur took Brian aside and did him the honour of pouring him a whisky.

Brian drank his health, and they were soon deep in conversation away from the noise and bustle of the dancers.

'And would you enjoy an occasional opportunity to go to sea, then, Brian?' Willie was saying in a casual tone.

'I wouldn't mind, if there was a chance.'

'As well as leaving the lifeboat, I was wanting to be less tied to the fishing,' Willie went on. 'A standby crewman would be a great thing. Maybe if I didn't want to go out, or a man was ill, would you be interested in the job?'

'It sounds like an answer to a prayer, Willie. I'd be thankful to have the chance to pick up some extra cash. Do you think I could do it?'

'Ay, you could do it, and fit the croft work round it. The money would make a difference right enough.'

'It would make all the difference!'

'What about your wife?' Willie enquired.

'I'm afraid she won't take too kindly to it. I haven't explained to her yet how short of money we're going to be. I'll accept your offer, Willie. I'll be glad to. It's an answer to my problems.'

'I'm glad you're agreeable, lad. I know you'll fit in with the rest of the boys. Anyway, you'll be able to tell that lovely wife of yours all about it. Here she comes!'

'Well, look, if you don't mind,' Brian answered awkwardly, 'I'd like to choose my moment. You know what women can be like!'

'And what exactly do you mean by that remark?' Fiona asked brightly as she reached them, and raised wide eyes in mock alarm.

Willie bowed in greeting to her.

'Oh, it's nothing to worry about.' Brian playfully offered his wife his arm. 'May I escort you to supper, my fair lady?'

As she walked back towards the buffet, Fiona shot Brian a look of vague unease.

★ ★ ★

The morning after the party, Eileen's alarm clock shattered her dawn sleep.

She was exhausted; physically and emotionally drained after the events of the evening and Rhona Morrison's offer. She had to get out of bed. She must get breakfast for Shona and Dad.

Eileen caught sight of herself in the mirror as she hastily tied her dressing-gown round her slim figure. She made her way downstairs thinking of how Duncan's arm had seemed warm, and so right, about her shoulders last night and, when he'd folded her against his chest to kiss her gently, she'd felt herself melt into his embrace with a new longing, and surrender her lips to his with a strange hunger.

When she reached the kitchen she switched on the kettle and the grill and, just as she put some bread to toast, she suddenly knew. The decision seemed to be made for her, and to come from outside herself. She would go to London; Shona would just have to take over the running of the house.

A kind of peace settled on her now that the decision had been made. Just then Shona, wrapped in a pink cotton dressing-gown, came drifting through the living-room, scuffling the heels of her mules along. Her cheeks were still flushed with sleep, her hair tumbled about her face. She looked like a drowsy child.

'Morning, Eileen!' was followed by a huge yawn. 'I'm bushed.'

'So am I. Here's some coffee, Shona. It'll wake you up.'

'I suppose we'll have to go along to the hall and finish clearing up?'

'Yep.'

'I can't. I'm shattered.' A coaxing look was sent to her sister and a dimple indented one round cheek as she sighed heavily.

Eileen tried to ignore her sister's appealing

looks. They'd melt the heart of a villain.

'Dad still asleep?'

'Yes. I'm letting him lie in.'

They sat down with their coffee cups.

'I saw you having a great confab with Julia and Mrs Morrison last night,' Shona ventured.

'Oh, yes. It's exciting. I've got something to tell you . . . ' Eileen was interrupted by the noisy rattle of the letterbox. 'That'll waken Dad,' she said, jumping up.

But Shona, seemingly forgetting her lethargy, shot in front of her, reached the lobby first and gathered up the mail.

'There's one for you. A bill.' She widened her eyes comically and handed a brown envelope to her sister. 'And . . . one for me! It's from Glasgow!'

Boredom and discontent vanished from her face as though a light had been switched on. Excitedly, she tore open the envelope and scanned the scrawled pages.

'Yippee! Tony's found me a place to stay. It's a flat with two other girls!' Shona shook her head as though she could hardly take in her good fortune. Flopping into the armchair, she stared at the opposite wall, as at a film screen on which she could see all the colour and activity of a new life opening up for her.

'The only stumbling block is Dad. He'll go spare!' She leaned forward impetuously, towards her sister. 'Look, Eileen, you've got to back me up. I don't just want to go away. I must go. I'll die here! I know you understand. Help me with Dad!'

Eileen stared at her sister as though she was slightly out of focus. Her mind was in a turmoil again. Thoughts too complicated to unravel raced and entwined in her brain. There would inevitably be a scene with their father when Shona dropped her bombshell. Only her own intervention could help her young sister. And Shona did need to get away. Instinctively, Eileen had always accepted this.

'You go, Shona,' she said at last, no shadow of what it cost her showing in her face. 'I'll help you.'

Eileen's Anguish

As Julia Macpherson made her way to the village hall later that Saturday morning, she felt at peace with her world. Willie's retiral party had been a success, and she'd played her part in making it so. Willie was a valued friend. In fact, he was the one person in whose company she always felt entirely at ease; while her feelings of concern for the welfare of Eileen and Shona fell little short of those of a mother.

That was why, in spite of being a little tired, she had this pleasant sense of purpose.

She found the hall door unlocked but, to her surprise, no sign of the girls.

In no time, she had thoroughly swept the floor. She went to fetch a shovel to gather up the debris into a bucket, suddenly anxious to have the hall immaculate again, and ready for its next invasion. She paused near the front of the hall, thinking that she'd heard something coming from the small committee room nearby. It sounded almost eerie, like a gasp or a sob.

Julia stood listening for a moment. There was definitely someone in there. Somebody sobbing! She moved softly towards the door, peered through and froze.

Eileen was there: a lovely, desolate figure, unaware of anyone else's presence. She was slumped over the table, her head on her arms, and hard, hurting sobs were shaking her body. She would hate it if she thought anyone had witnessed the crumpling of her composure Julia told herself, and edged backwards from the door until, crash! She stumbled against the bucket, toppling it over with a resounding clatter, which echoed round the empty hall.

The sobs were choked off and replaced by a listening silence.

'Oh, drat!' Julia said in a normal voice, furious with herself for her clumsiness, but improvising as best she could. Humming then, as though she thought she was alone, she went on noisily righting the bucket and brushing up around it.

A few moments later Eileen emerged from the room.

'Hello, Julia!' She was smiling a bright, forced smile.

'Oh, there you are, Eileen!' Julia feigned surprise.

Eileen's tears had been wiped away and she started chattering about the events of the party.

Julia was not deceived. Something was seriously amiss. Perhaps Eileen and Duncan had fallen out?

When the girl ran out of her hectic patter, Julia eagerly voiced the question she'd been longing to ask.

'Will you be leaving us soon, then, Eileen? Setting off for London?' Julia slid the last of the dust into the bucket.

'No.' Eileen looked away quickly.

'But, Eileen . . . I thought that . . . '

'I'm not going, Julia,' the girl began hesitantly. 'I realise I just haven't got what it takes.'

'Eileen!' Julia let the shovel drop into the bucket. 'It's impossible to be objective about yourself. Others have made that judgment for you. We know you have exactly what it takes,' she said confidently.

'No, I haven't, Julia, and besides, I couldn't leave Dad,' Eileen blurted out. 'I'm needed here. Oh, don't say any more about it. I've made up my mind. I'm staying here!'

Julia recalled the girl's bright eagerness about the project only the night before, and became more convinced than ever that something had intervened to cause this change of heart.

Surely Willie hadn't blocked his daughter's chances? Or Duncan thrown a spanner in?

70

She couldn't imagine either case.

'Wait a day or two, yet,' Julia told her firmly, determined to find out the truth behind this amazing turn-about. 'A day or two won't matter,' she coaxed. 'Keep an open mind.'

★ ★ ★

His eyes narrowed against the sparkle of the water, Willie McArthur watched his fishing boat, the Stella Maris, head out to sea, with a younger man taking his place at the wheel.

Willie had thought he'd feel nothing but relief when he'd sent the young lads off without him. But there was no feeling at all — only an emptiness. Various people called out and waved to him as he made his way home. He tried to ignore the hollowness inside him and smartened up his step as though he had a purpose ahead of him — just up the road.

He was a fine-looking man. Although his hair was grizzled now, it was still thick, rising off his brow in small, crinkling waves. His eyes were maybe a less-bright blue than they had once been, but they could still twinkle merrily when he was amused. His habit of screwing them up against glare had caused lines to fan out from the corners. His laughter lines, Shona called them.

Shona could make him laugh. He thought of her as he surged up the road with the purposeful stride he'd put on for his neighbours. He hoped she'd be in. If she was in, she'd amuse him, bring him a cup of tea, maybe.

'Thank you, God, for Shona!' He said a brief prayer. It was a habit he'd got into at sea. 'For my two girls,' he amended hastily.

God, am I really too old? he thought to himself. The doctor said I should retire. I've got to leave the lifeboat crew. That's the new 'age' rule. But, the Stella Maris — my own boat?

Maybe a rest's all I need. I'm glad they've asked me to be the new honorary secretary of the lifeboat. That'll keep me in touch . . .

He called to Shona and Eileen when he went in, but they were both out. His big, worn chair felt good, but not half as good as it had after a hard night's fishing. He decided to read the paper, but couldn't find his glasses. Never mind. He leaned back.

He was wakened an hour later by a gentle tugging at his feet. Still dazed by sleep, he half-opened his eyes.

'Dad, I've wakened you! I didn't mean to!'

'Shona! Bless you! I thought you were your mother for a moment.'

'You've been dreaming, Dad. I thought you'd be more comfortable with your boots off.'

'Light of my eyes! You're the best wee boot-jack a man ever had!' He smiled.

Shona had been performing this duty since her childhood days.

He sighed contentedly. Peace descended on him, and wordlessly his broad hand went out to stroke his daughter's bright hair. His touch was a moth's kiss, as though he touched something infinitely precious. She was her mother over again.

Shona looked back at her father, her blue eyes filled with affection, and there was no sound in the room but the ticking of the old clock on the wall.

At last, still kneeling in front of him, she said again, 'I didn't mean to disturb you.'

'You're not disturbing me, lass. You're just looking after me like you've always done. I'm a lucky man. I don't know what I'd do if I didn't have you and Eileen!'

'Dad.' Shona looked anywhere but into his eyes. She lifted his boots away to the back premises and returned and sat in the opposite chair. 'I've something to tell you.'

Willie moved uneasily.

'I'm going away from here to live in Glasgow!' she announced.

The news hit Willie like a blow from an iron bludgeon. For a moment it deprived him of breath. The hollow feeling rushed back — the emptiness.

Shona waited, poised to brave the storm about to descend on her.

It never came.

Her eyes grew round with wonder and her bottom lip pouted endearingly, ready for battle then pursed a little in puzzlement.

'Dad?' she ventured at last, almost pleading with him to unleash his thunderbolts at her and get it over. But still Willie showed no anger.

Indeed he seemed, as the long seconds ticked by, to manage to wipe all expression from his face. And his voice, when he spoke, was unnaturally soft and husky.

'I was not expecting you to look after me all your life,' he said with a kind of pride that was nearly Shona's undoing.

'If your wish is to stay in Glasgow — ' he made it sound like the last place on earth anyone would wish to stay ' — then go. Just go.'

Shona's mouth opened, but no words came.

'Eileen and I will manage fine . . . without

74

you,' Willie continued, his voice cracking.

Shona swallowed over a huge lump in her throat. She'd have much preferred anger and threats. Oh, why was life so difficult at times?

She got up and went to put the kettle on, blinking hard. She was determined not to cry, reminding herself that she was the one who never cried. Never.

When she'd gone, Willie's head fell back against the padded leather. He knew that the colour had drained out of his face. He could feel the cold clamminess on his brow. He hoped Shona would bring the tea soon for he knew he couldn't get up and face things yet — not just yet . . .

★ ★ ★

Fiona was surprised to see Agnes Campbell approaching Rowanlea. She was walking up the track from the road, carrying a shopping bag, and accompanied by two young children.

Fiona went out to meet them.

'I've brought them to see the new chicks,' Agnes announced. 'I've none at the moment. They're my niece's children, Samantha and Jamie, here for a wee holiday.'

The young child, the girl, had her hair

drawn into two little pleats by a firm hand, possibly Agnes's, leaving a pale, small face rather wide eyed and unprotected looking.

The boy was about two years older and was already hopping from one foot to the the other, impatient to be moving on. He was a bright, snub-nosed child, pale, too, but with a sprinkling of freckles across his nose and cheeks, warming them.

'They've both had flu, and we're going to get the roses back in their cheeks,' Agnes said brightly.

'Come on, then!' Fiona took Samantha's hand and, with Jamie hopping and skipping beside them, they made their way to the stretch of grass where Brian had put the chicken-run, with its own little house at one end.

The children were enchanted and started poking grass-stalks through, to attract the fluffy creatures to the wire.

'Pity you hadn't come a little earlier. We used to have a wee kitten.' Fiona's eyes darkened momentarily. 'But I'm afraid we had to find a new home for him.'

Dr Frazer had insisted that Nicky the kitten should go, as he was convinced the animal had an adverse effect on Fiona's asthmatic condition.

After admiring the chickens for a while

Jamie decided that he'd go and explore for a change.

'They'll be all right on their own, won't they?' Fiona asked anxiously.

'Perfectly,' Agnes Campbell assured her.

'Then let's go in and I'll put the kettle on.'

Agnes followed Fiona into the house. It was her first visit, so accordingly she'd brought a present. She reached into her shopper and produced a parcel that contained a Dundee cake.

'It's perfect,' Fiona admired the cake. 'I wish I could bake like that.'

'It's just practice, and you'll get plenty of that.' Agnes smiled.

She took a seat by the fire. Her brown hair was streaked with grey and scraped severely back into a knot. Her sharp, black eyes seemed to dart about taking everything in.

As they drank their tea, her gaze kept coming back to Fiona.

'How are you settling in, then?' It was kindly asked, for Agnes sensed some tension and worry in the girl.

'We're settling in all right, I think. It's just . . . ' Fiona hesitated. Her mind reached for some way to alter what she was about to say. 'I didn't realise how tight money was going to be.' Her face reddened and she stared into the fire.

'Yes.' Agnes nodded. 'We're none of us very flush for money hereabouts.'

'But Brian's accepted an offer from Mr McArthur for a place on the boat!' Fiona informed her.

'He's away out on the Stella Maris, is he?'

'Yes.' Fiona sighed.

'Well, Duncan goes to the fishing. Crofters often do. You have to allow men their independence,' Agnes said quietly.

'I think Brian's doing it for the money. Because we're short . . . ' Fiona began, feeling a little embarrassed.

'Of course he is. Why else? He wants to provide for you. Don't take away his pride in doing that!'

'But . . . I wish I could help. I feel so useless . . . '

'Well.' Agnes studied Fiona appraisingly. 'You look a bright girl. We've a craft shop in the village, we open in the summer. What can you do?' She put her empty teacup down. 'Just about every woman here can knit, or crochet, or sew. As well as my baking and preserving, I make goat's cheese.'

Fiona leaned forward eagerly. 'When do you open the shop?'

'The beginning of next month. We take turns at tending it. All the women who can manage give a morning or an afternoon.'

Fiona's eyes had brightened. An idea was forming in her mind but before she had time to voice it they were suddenly interrupted.

'Can we take a chick home, Aunt Agnes?' Samantha burst in the back door, sending a beseeching look to her great-aunt.

'No, you can't take the wee soul away from its mummy, Samantha.'

'But you can come back and see them whenever you like,' Fiona comforted her. 'Would you like some biscuits?'

Samantha nodded, and was soon running out to join her brother, taking a 'picnic' with her.

Fiona gave Agnes a second cup of tea, and they settled down again.

'Do you know where I could get lots of wool or yarn cheaply, Mrs Campbell?'

'I know where you could get bags full of unwanted wool for nothing — from the knitters around here. And there's the knitwear factory up the loch. They might have scraps which they could let you have. Then there's the advertisements you see in the magazines . . . Were you going to knit?' Agnes nodded in approval. 'Good for you!'

Fiona looked back at her, smiling, happy and purposeful.

'No. Not knit. I've got a hand-loom.'

A few days later the children were back, this time carrying small bags of corn to feed the chickens.

'I want to catch a chicken.' Samantha confided in Brian, whom the children had come on, busy in his new vegetable garden.

'Do you, pet?' Brian smiled, enchanted by the small face turned confidingly up to him. He put down the hoe he was using, and knelt down beside her. Jamie promptly climbed on his back and demanded a piggy-back.

Their squeals of laughter reached Fiona, working in the kitchen.

What antics were they up to? She went to the window.

Brian's head was thrown back. His face was wiped free of all strain — and he was laughing merrily. She couldn't remember when she'd seen him so carefree. He was so animated and alive.

Fiona caught her breath.

Brian swung Samantha, squealing with delight, into the air, then set her down again like a flushed and happy little doll.

Fiona almost felt her heart flipping over, and at the same time, an inner voice was whispering, this is the man I love. He needs a child of his own!

'No matter what the doctors say,' she whispered to herself, 'I'm going to have a baby for him!'

'That's Your Style'

A fresh breeze, as well as her determination, had whipped colour into Julia Macpherson's cheeks as she made her way along to the McArthurs'.

Willie welcomed her thankfully, just realising, when he saw her standing on his doorstep, how much he needed someone to talk to. Julia was a good listener. As she sat down, the room seemed warmed by her presence.

Willie sank back into his chair, comforted, to regard the steady eyes that looked out at his world with such compassion.

'Have you heard, then, Julia?' He folded his arms and leaned back. 'Fancy that girl wanting to go away from here! Did you ever hear of such a daft notion?'

Julia lifted her head and gazed at him incredulously. Utter dismay gripped her. She wondered if she was hearing right.

Her eyes clouded over for a moment, before she frowned and looked away, only half-accepting the terrible thought that Willie could spoil his daughter's chances.

Her mind began to reach desperately for

all the arguments she had marshalled there, should they be needed. They stood inside her like a row of soldiers ready for battle.

Now it was time to rally them, and lead them out.

'Willie!' She leaned towards him. 'Eileen must grasp this London opportunity with both hands! It could never happen again! It's a once-in-a-lifetime chance. She's earned it. She deserves it. She needs it!' Her voice was rising. 'Far from being a daft notion . . . ' She took a great gulp of air. 'It's a wonderful opportunity!'

'Eileen?' Willie broke in at last, almost peevishly. 'What are you havering about, woman? It's Shona I'm speaking about! She's going away to Glasgow. Just leaving me and Eileen behind!' His voice was bleak and his eyes had lost their glow.

'So that's it!' Julia compressed her lips. Suddenly everything became clear, heart-wrenchingly clear. The painful memory of Eileen sobbing quietly came back to her.

'Willie. It's not Shona you should be letting go — it's Eileen.'

'Eileen!'

'Yes. She probably won't tell you now, but she's been offered an opportunity to study music in London. She's turned it down. It must be because of Shona. She's

83

convinced herself that her place is here, looking after you!'

Willie was holding the arms of his chair, his face a study of conflicting emotions.

'Eileen? Eileen wants to go, too?'

'Yes, Willie. And you mustn't let her miss this chance. Hers is a rare talent,' Julia implored him breathlessly, her eyes pleading.

Willie sat dazed, his head in his hands now, a storm of mixed feeling sweeping over him.

Julia was exhausted. She still felt a smothered sense of frustration. Had she said enough to convince him?

Suddenly she shivered. She had the sensation that there was another presence in the room, the sound of a soft breath behind her. She turned sharply, just as Willie looked up.

A white-faced Shona was standing just inside the door. She'd been listening and she'd heard every impassioned word.

'Oh, no!' she cried, her eyes stricken. 'She never told me. She should have told me!'

'I'm sorry you heard it like that, Shona.' Julie looked at her with pity. 'But it's true.'

Shona found it an oddly-disturbing glance, loving, but unsmiling.

'What will you do, Dad?' she whispered.

Willie shrugged helplessly and Julia's

mouth tightened, but neither of them spoke.

'I'll not go,' Shona said suddenly, her eyes glistening with tears she would not shed. 'I'll stay here. Eileen deserves this chance, and — somebody has to look after you, Dad.'

'Maybe it's for the best, *mo ghaoil*. Maybe your destiny lies here, in Achnacraig, right enough.

'Julia . . . ' He turned his head. The serious eyes beneath the wide brow were level with his. He saw something there that disturbed him. 'You're right, of course, Eileen must be given her chance. Shona and I will just have to manage somehow.'

He was unprepared for her reaction.

Julia's eyes blazed. She rose, drawing herself up tall.

★ ★ ★

'I've heard enough of this selfish nonsense of yours, Willie,' she began, speaking firmly and deliberately, 'and I'm fed up with it. Where's your commonsense?'

'Commonsense?' Willie looked up at her, bewildered. 'I thought I was showing commonsense. I just want what's best — '

'Of course you do,' she interrupted vehemently. 'You want the best for everybody. Everybody — but most of all yourself!'

85

'Don't be hard, Julia,' he pleaded in his soft brogue, nearly undoing her.

She took hold of his hands and gripped them tightly.

'Look, Willie, I'm here!'

He regarded her plaintively but she wouldn't let him charm her.

'I'm only three doors away — '

From a caring, helpful neighbour and friend, she'd taken on the possessiveness of a — Willie's thoughts jammed.

Julia then turned to Shona with all the protectiveness of a mother tiger. 'Don't you worry, Shona. He'll be fine. Both you and Eileen can get on with your lives. It's time your father stopped feeling sorry for himself and pulled himself together.'

Julia hadn't finished with Willie.

'You're not helpless, are you?' she goaded. 'You're not an old man?' That did it.

'Of course not,' he denied sharply.

'Well, it's time you learned to look after yourself.'

'You're right, Julia. We can't argue with her, can we, Shona?' He turned his beguiling eyes back to Julia. 'I was just a bit taken aback by the suddenness. By them both wanting to go away at once.' He looked at Julia, noticing her flushed cheeks and bright eyes and momentarily he felt a flicker of some crazy emotion he'd thought never to feel again.

Then suddenly Julia moved away quickly towards the door.

'Hey! Where are you going?' Willie cried.

Shona stretched out her hand to detain her.

Julia had pulled the door open.

'That's you two sorted out,' she called over her shoulder to them. 'I'm away to do the same for Eileen. She'll be down at Insharroch Bay with Duncan as sure as fate. Cheerio!' With a soft closing of the door, she was gone.

★ ★ ★

Fiona realised, with a sense of wonder, that she was experiencing a quiet contentment, a kind of peace.

She was sitting, weaving at her loom near the window. It was evening, but the light lingered long in the Highlands.

'These are very attractive,' Agnes Campbell had said, when she'd seen the first few luncheon mats completed. They were black with silver lurex threads shining through, and greeny-yellow border motifs of stylised pine trees.

'Glamorous is the word for them,' she'd

declared. She'd examined the fringing and the careful finish. 'Most professional! I expect you have to do everything with that perfection. That's your style!'

Fiona smiled to herself. She hadn't been sure it was meant to be a compliment, an observation, or maybe a criticism. But, she had to admit that she hated to be associated with anything that was badly done. In between the various chores, she'd been spending as much time as possible weaving. It was satisfying to see the work grow, and the rhythm of it was soothing.

After a while she realised that she was straining her eyes. It was getting late. She rose and switched on the light. It would act, too, as a beacon to welcome Brian on his way home.

Brian was out on a lifeboat exercise. Not only did he put in fairly regular appearances at the fishing, but also, when asked, he'd accepted a place in the lifeboat crew.

Fiona sighed. He had been completely absorbed into the community. His only handicap, she thought wryly, was his wife's inability to match his gift for mixing.

She hadn't been too well. Two asthma attacks. The second one not so severe. It was nice to be busy, and happily waiting for your husband to come home.

The first set of mats completed, she was working on a new design. They were to be Christmas mats — red with white snowflake-patterned borders. She was really excited about them. She hadn't dreamed, when she'd taken weaving as one of her crafts at teacher training college, that it was going to hold so much fascination for her.

She didn't like it when Brian was so late. It was awful to love someone so much.

Hours seemed to pass before she heard the car. She knew the sound of it. In the stillness it could always be heard, long before it appeared on the high stretch of road. In no time the hatchback would be turning up the track. She left the loom and ran to the kitchen to switch on the kettle.

He came in, glowing and healthy from the exercise, scattering her doubts and fears before his magnificent, muscled presence.

Utterly secure again, laughing, she threw herself into his out-stretched arms, light-headed with relief and love.

'My!' he exclaimed. 'Are you glad to see me, then?'

'Yes!' she declared happily. 'D'you want tea?'

'I've just had some at the shed,' he told her. 'Oh, it's lovely, lovely to be home — and you're lovely!' He kissed her cheek.

She clung to him and his pulse leapt.

'I'm exhausted,' he said, 'and I've such a lot on tomorrow.'

'Go to bed,' she told him softly.

'I know. I must.'

She released him and he shrugged out of his jacket and stretched and yawned.

'I'm so tired,' he repeated, catching her again as she passed him, tidying up the room. He pulled her against him. 'At least I thought I was.'

They laughed together, happiness flowing in them like wine. And a strange excitement began to churn in her.

'Go on — go to bed.' She was smiling, nursing her inner excitement. His eyes caressed her, and a shiver ran down her spine.

'Go on — I won't be long.'

He left her, but only to go and get ready for bed — and to long for her to hurry up and join him.

When she slipped in beside him, Brian's arms wound round her hungrily.

'I love you, Fiona. I love you, darling,' he murmured.

They clung together as though they hadn't seen each other for months.

* * *

90

Goodbye, Dad!' Shona had given two weeks' notice to the hairdresser she'd assisted on the days he came to the hotel. And now she was ready to leave Achnacraig.

Willie feasted his eyes on her. This final look would have to last him for a long time.

Eileen was driving her to Fort William to join the Glasgow bus. She was going to miss her sister — the house would be dead without her scatty presence.

Shona leaned forward and gave her father a peck on the cheek. She could scarcely speak for the aching lump that rose in her throat. Hastily she got into the car and wound down the window.

'Cheerio!' She gulped.

'God bless you, *mo ghaoil*.' Willie had to turn away and blink at the sea. Although he'd made up his mind not to vex Shona by being emotional, he felt shaken.

Tony was waiting. Shona saw him first and felt uncertain. It was several weeks since she'd seen him. He was standing under the awning at Buchanan Street Bus Station, at just the point where the Citylink would pull in.

She waved shyly as she followed the driver to the luggage-hold to retrieve her bags, and then he was beside her.

'These yours?' He took charge of the two blue suit-cases and led her off to where he'd parked. The rain was sheeting down, so that they hardly spoke till the cases were stowed again, and they were inside the car.

'Well.' Tony threw his coat on to the back seat and brushed plastered hair from his brow. 'Haven't changed your mind?'

Shona shook her head, smiling through raindrops.

'No,' she assured him.

He put the car into gear.

The façades of hotels, shops and restaurants were lit up, their lights dazzling in the rain. Oh, it was beautiful! Shona felt she could have driven round just gazing at everything all night.

Too soon, it seemed, they reached her flat. She didn't know where she was. Near a bridge with handsome lamps on the parapet.

Tony parked his car in the street and led her back to a tenement building, four storeys high. They climbed three double flights of stairs then Tony stopped at a door with several name-cards inset above the bell.

Someone answered his ring.

'Maisie — I've brought Shona,' he announced to the girl who opened the door.

She was a small girl with short, black hair,

and really disreputable slippers on her feet. After greetings had been exchanged, she shuffled in front of them.

'Dump the cases a minute and come into the kitchen. We're not quite finished.'

They followed her into a bare, starkly-lit room. It was large, with ample room for a table and a number of chairs to the left of a gas cooker. There was a sink unit under the window and cupboards along one wall, leaving a large expanse of vinyl-covered floor.

'This is Vivien, Shona.' Maisie introduced the two girls.

'Hello!' Vivien quickly finished the remains of a fish supper. She was tall, very well groomed, and with an unmistakable style about her. 'Jane's out, but you'll meet her later,' she told Shona.

Jane was Tony's particular friend.

'Sit down. Would you like a cup of tea?'

Soon all four were seated round the table drinking tea from mugs.

'You'll have to get your own mug,' Maisie told her.

The two girls were neither unfriendly nor effusive, just very matter-of-fact. It was decided that Tony would go out for two more fish suppers, while Shona was shown round the flat.

Vivien gave her a run-down of the flat rules. She handled the rent which she got from the others, and paid, monthly in advance, to the landlady. They shared the light and gas bills as well as the television and phone rentals.

'You pay for any calls you make over and above. There's a book beside the phone. Don't forget to mark them in,' Vivien warned.

It was all very strange. Shona had never had to worry about money in her entire life. Her father had insisted on giving her a sum of money, and on getting her a cheque book of her own.

'You can't be drawing large amounts, like your rent will be, and walking about the city with it in your handbag,' he'd pointed out.

He was going to be proved right about something else, she surmised. When she had thanked him for being so generous, he'd said, 'It won't last long. If you can't get work, you'll just have to come home.'

'I know, Dad,' she'd replied, but she'd resolved not to be forced to return home. Somehow she would have to find employment.

* * *

After Shona and Tony had eaten and tidied up, they joined the girls who'd gone to watch

94

a favourite TV programme.

It was the first time Shona had observed Tony in relation to other people he knew better than she did. He had such an air of confidence and certainty about all that he said and did, that she felt a strange sense of awe.

She couldn't look at him without remembering their magical time together on the West Coast, and wondering if she'd imagined their mutual attraction.

Vivien switched off the television when the programme came to an end. It was as though Tony had been waiting for this cue to speak.

'Shona, I know you're desperate for work and — believe it or not — Vivien thinks she might be able to help you.' He turned to his tall, elegant friend. 'Will you tell her, Viv?'

'I'm a buyer in one of the large department stores in town.' Vivien turned languidly towards Shona. 'Tony's been pestering us for ideas for you. But I couldn't say anything until I had seen you . . . Now that I have — there's a possibility.'

She paused and studied Shona as though she was assessing her.

'Frankly — ' She laughed ruefully. 'It's because you're so ridiculously good looking that it might work.'

'We didn't believe Tony,' Maisie put in with a humorous grimace. 'It's not fair!' She had an infectious laugh, and a habit of putting her oar in with a lively wit when Vivien was speaking.

'Well,' the older girl resumed, 'in my store, my best friend is in charge of Cosmetics. She's just lost an assistant. The silly cookie went on holiday to Greece, met a Greek, and isn't coming back.'

'It's unbelievable, isn't it?' Maisie exclaimed.

Vivien ignored the interruption.

'There are scores of girls waiting for these opportunities. There's a training scheme, and normally you wouldn't have a chance, but . . . I know my friend, and — given two qualities that you have — I think she would, at least, be interested in seeing you.'

'What are they?' Maisie asked.

'One, those extraordinary looks, with that complexion! And, two, she's got the most precise diction I've ever heard!'

Tony decided he could leave Shona now. They were deep in a discussion about make-up when Shona got up to see him out.

'Shona, let me know how you get on.'

'I will,' she assured him. 'And, Tony, I'll never be able to thank you.' She was suddenly shy and her shyness seemed to affect him.

'See you!' he sketched a salute, turned, and ran down the stairs.

* * *

Here, Hamish. Will you hold these, please?' Julia Macpherson called to one of the red-haired McRorys to hold a pile of books as she opened the school door. A few minutes later she rang the bell, and got the score of squealers to line up in the playground.

She didn't like to have them entering the schoolroom any-old-how. It was better to start the day with quiet orderliness, then everything went more smoothly. Soon the twenty children were in the room. They ranged in age from five to eleven.

There had been sixty children in the school when Julia had started and she'd had an assistant. Like all villages, you got odd birth-patterns. For instance, there was only one four-year-old going to enter school in August. And, oddly, there were five children, this year, aged eleven, about to go away to secondary school.

She would miss those five bright buttons. They were clever and helpful. It was almost like having friends around. Still, the others were coming on. She studied their solemn faces. Fancy only one other coming to join them next year!

'We'll stop ten minutes before the interval and have a wee discussion. I think we should decide what to have for the end-of-term social. A few musical items? Would any of you recite a poem?'

No hands went up. But that was usual. The Highland children were shy. She would just have to persuade them.

'All right. We'll talk about it in a wee while. Carry on.'

She liked the summer term. Everything was more relaxed. The jars on the nature table were full of wild flowers, and tightly-packed bunches of bluebells crowned the chipped vases on the windowsills.

She had the children all round her, and a tentative list of items for an entertainment in her hand, when one of the Education Advisers arrived. He breezed in, after a brief knock — plump, grey haired, and wearing a suit which nicely combined his business calling with its country setting.

'We'll let them start their playtime now, Miss Macpherson,' he declared jovially, giving the children a benign smile. 'Off you go!' he commanded.

'And how are things?' he enquired as he gazed around the classroom.

She'd had the same conversation many times with him — and with his predecessor. He looked at the register, asked about reasons for absences; talked about the leavers. Through long practice, Julia was able to have half-an-ear on the playground sounds. Nothing untoward was happening. Still, it had been an awfully long interval — twenty minutes.

When it became half an hour, she became restive. She would have to excuse herself and check on the children; but before she'd a chance to do so, the man brought their meeting to a close at last.

'There's another family leaving the village, I hear,' he remarked off-handedly. 'The Galbraiths.'

'The Galbraiths?' Julia hadn't heard. She was shocked. There was a Galbraith boy in school, as well as a toddler at home. 'That'll make the roll . . . ?'

'Yes. Only fifteen.'

Julia's throat went dry.

'I'm afraid the school's scheduled for closure,' he continued, his smile strained.

Julia's knees gave way and she sat down abruptly, wiping her hands down over her face. What was she going to do?

A Secret Happiness

Julia never could remember how she got through the rest of the day of the education officer's visit. She must have performed all her duties, taken a lunch break, dismissed the children at four o'clock, and returned to the schoolhouse — all on 'automatic pilot.'

Eventually she'd found herself in her own bedroom with the door shut, alone with her thoughts. And the one appalling thought was uppermost in her mind — *They're going to close my school!*

She felt devastated — and ashamed of herself for feeling like that. Pushing the jumble of disconnected thoughts to the back of her mind, she forced herself to move briskly to the door. There was surely some work she could do.

Downstairs she attempted to do some marking but, from time to time, she'd find herself nervously twisting the red pencil round and round between her fingers, her eyes blank, her mind mulling over, again and again, what the adviser had told her.

He hadn't actually told her not to tell anyone until official notifications arrived, but she was sure she ought to keep silent for the moment. Besides, she didn't want to be the one to drop such a bombshell into the community.

The school had been there for a hundred years. Before that the children of the district had been taught in a small white-washed building on the same site. If only she could talk to someone, confide her fears and her anguish . . .

All week, the pain and worry never left her. They settled on her chest like a dull weight that wouldn't go away. Working hours were all right. She rediscovered the balm of having too much to do, no time to think. The evenings were the worst.

One evening, while she was out for a stroll, she heard the thump of the ceilidh band coming from the hall as she passed — but it all seemed remote from her, another world. She wandered home again, feeling more isolated and alone than ever. When she reached her front door she couldn't find her key. It was the last straw.

Weariness settled on her. She must have dashed out in such a hurry that she'd left her key inside. Both doors, and the downstairs windows, were shut. She'd have to go along to Eileen. She always kept a spare key for Julia.

Eileen was at the ceilidh. So the door was opened by Willie.

'Willie,' she began brightly. 'I'm such an idiot. I've lost my key . . . ' Then, to her utter dismay, two large tears began to roll down her cheeks, and the last words came out in a little sobbing wail. She realised, with horror, that it sounded as though she'd lost — not her key — but something infinitely precious and irreplaceable.

In the dusky light, Willie's eyes narrowed with concern. He took her arm, pulled her inside and shut the door.

'There, there, Julia.' He patted her shoulder. 'What is it? What is it you've lost?'

'I — I don't think I'm . . . supposed to tell you.' Julia tried to stifle her sobs.

Willie looked with dismay at the taut misery on her face, the shadows under her eyes, the faint hollows in her cheeks.

'I don't care what you've done. You've got to tell me,' he said, managing to sound both firm and concerned.

'Oh, Willie.' She smiled tremulously. 'I haven't done anything. It's just that they're going to close the school.'

Willie said nothing at first. He was stunned, shocked into silence. Then gradually he began to feel anger rising in him.

'The devil they are!' he told her fiercely.

His fury was balm to her wound. She nodded, unable to speak.

Willie put his arm round her tentatively at first, then more firmly.

'Och, don't cry, Julia. Don't cry, *mo ghaoil.*' His sympathy was so sweet and his soft, caressing voice so kind, that the unhappiness of the last week flooded over her, and she abandoned herself to his strong arms and wept against his shoulder.

For an endless, exquisite moment he held her, and then she fought against the desire to cling to him. She felt she had no right, and moved swiftly back.

He straightened himself and looked at her with a half-tender, half-reproving smile.

'Right, that's enough of this daft nonsense! Let's get our act together, as our Shona would say,' he said suddenly, and she burst into shaky, slightly-hysterical laughter.

It was ridiculous to hear that sort of mid-Atlantic slang being delivered in a soft, Highland brogue.

★ ★ ★

'Sit down, Julia. You're still overwrought,' Willie said firmly, as he took her arms and pressed her into a chair.

'Willie, I don't think it should be

103

mentioned till the official letters come to the parents.'

'No-one will hear it from me, Julia,' he said softly. 'There's just one thing that bothers me, though,' he went on. 'Why did you keep it to yourself for so long — getting more and more agitated?' His arctic-blue eyes regarded her keenly. 'Do you not know that you should share such worry with a trusted friend? I'm hurt that you didn't come to me at once.'

'I should have. I just never thought. I should have come to you right away. I feel better already . . . What — what should I d . . . do, Willie?'

He leaned forward from the opposite chair, took her free hand and squeezed it gently. When he smiled she felt the pull of his attraction. It wasn't going to solve the underlying problem, but she found herself coming slowly alive again. She wouldn't have thought it possible an hour earlier.

'Just sit there,' Willie said comfortingly. 'We've all the time in the world — and we'll talk about it . . . '

★ ★ ★

It was late June. The days had been fine and the croft work was well advanced. Duncan

104

Campbell left the house by the back door, sped up the side of the small, cultivated fields, and dropped down into the glen where the burn flowed.

All his life he'd had the sound of the rushing brown water in his ears and, ever since he could run, he'd run to it. He couldn't have told anyone what made him come here. It was some instinct.

Maybe it was the call of one of the rhythms in his blood. There was the rhythm of the land, the rhythm of the sea, and the rhythm of the burn.

As a boy, after a spate, he had spent many hours sitting on his favourite rock, as still as a statue, looking into a deep, rock-lined pool, searching for the presence of trout or a salmon.

He sat on his rock now, staring into the water, sensing the feeling of exultation that his lithe body and his fitness, the bright air and the rushing water always gave him. The poetry of it was inside him, straining for release like the water, but he could never express it in words. It was the same when he looked at Eileen. He could never tell her what she meant to him . . .

He heard someone coming up the path on the other side of the burn, the path that came from the roadway. Like an eel he slid away and silently faded into the trees, but as the footsteps grew nearer he recognised their soft tread and, hardly daring to hope, he turned round. He caught his breath — it was Eileen!

For a moment he didn't know what to do. Should he call to her or leave her alone? He didn't want to frighten her, but he longed to speak to her.

She stopped on the grassy stretch opposite where he'd been, and stared up at the high bank over which lay his croft.

'Duncan!' she called softly.

A warm feeling of relief came over him as he came out of his hiding place, smiling across at her.

'I thought you'd be somewhere about!' She laughed. She looked cool in a green and white summer dress, and her arms, face and neck were a warm, creamy tan.

He lightly crossed the rocks to her side and put his arm round her shoulder. Then they continued up the path beside the burn. It was the path that walkers used, the peat-cutters, and the climbers who wanted to penetrate to the mountains beyond. Neither questioned why or how the other happened to be there.

'Well, what's the news of Shona?' Duncan asked.

Her reaction to his question surprised him. She seemed awkward, agitated somehow. Her words, however, didn't tie in with her behaviour.

'Shona? Oh, she's getting on fine — at least as far as I know. As a matter of fact, I was thinking that, instead of getting the London train from Inverness, I would go through Glasgow on the way.'

'Good thinking. You're thick as thieves, you two. It's all arranged, then? You'll soon be away?' He wondered how he could sound so matter-of-fact, so politely interested, when he felt as if a knife was turning in his heart. He lifted a stick and whacked ferociously at the bracken.

Eileen was hardly aware of what he was doing, too many thoughts were racing through her head. Maybe he doesn't care at all. I don't know if I can stand being away from him. What if I came back and he was married to someone else?

'I'll be away in three weeks,' she said calmly, trying to keep a grip on herself. 'I'm to stay with Professor and Mrs Padenski in Hampstead. He'll give me lots of extra tuition, you see, and advice.'

'Well, I'm glad there's going to be someone to look after you,' Duncan remarked.

'It doesn't strike you that I'm quite well

107

able to look after myself?'

He stopped, threw away the stick with which he'd flattened yards of bracken, and took her hands in his.

'You're not letting yourself be forced into all this London business, are you?' he said, looking down at her with serious eyes.

'Duncan Campbell! That's just like you. Of course I'm not being forced. I'm choosing it. Can't you see? I'm choosing to go. I want to . . .'

'You do? Then I want you to go, too,' he said with a sigh. 'If that's what'll make you happy.'

If only he would say, *I don't want you to go.*

On an impulse, Eileen slipped her arm through his.

'You know, you are absurd . . . You don't know what you want . . .'

But I do, I do, he thought in anguish. *I want you, Eileen* — if only I was one of those blokes who could just say it. I LOVE YOU!

Instead he said, 'This east wind has been just grand for the peats. They're dry as dry. I must be away up to the hags tomorrow.'

And the romantic moment was gone.

Eileen pulled her arm away and tossed her head with a gesture reminiscent of Shona.

Frustration was rising up in her, but she was determined not to show it.

'I'll race you to the stile,' she called, flying off with her hair streaming.

It was an old wooden stile, weathered to the same grey as the dry-stane dyke it straddled.

They reached it together and he caught her breathless body in his arms and kissed her.

As always, she melted beneath his touch, held in his arms by a compelling tenderness. As always, his arms, hands and lips seemed to tell her of his love, but he never spoke the words she wanted to hear.

'Could you live in the town, Duncan?' She whispered the question in the circle of his arms. She wanted to know the answer.

'Ach, no. Never!'

'Och,' was soft, considering, but 'Ach,' was rejection, utter repudiation with a touch of hostility. She knew now.

She would go. It was all arranged. It seemed to be her fate to go. And she might never come back.

Duncan looked down at her face, like a flower, still held gently against his arm, and thought his heart would break.

★ ★ ★

As the summer wore on, Fiona came to enjoy taking her turn in the craft shop. She was getting to know the other women, especially those who contributed goods and helped in the shop. This had been a busy day.

Before she'd come in she'd been to visit Dr Frazer, at his surgery, and she was bubbling over with a fierce, secret happiness.

She helped some tourists to make choices of matching Fair-Isle bonnets and scarves. Her own good taste was generally useful to customers.

One of the other helpers, who sat knitting when she wasn't required to serve, asked her advice about combining certain colours in a garment, with a friendly naturalness that surprised her.

Fiona was discovering that, where people would be shy of coming to your door, they would pop into the craft shop for a word any time.

'Almost time for a cup of tea, Mrs McNeil. I'll put the kettle on!' Fiona announced after giving her advice.

Mrs McNeil finished counting her stitches.

'I'll make it,' she called, as the shop doorbell pinged again, and more tourists entered.

Although occasionally Fiona seemed to be gazing into space, a secret smile playing about her lips, the afternoon sped past. When the time came to close the shop, she was glad to see Brian along in the village with the car, to give her a run home.

'How did you get on with the doctor?' he asked as they drove off.

Fiona's heart jumped. But he was talking about her asthma.

'Oh, fine,' she answered him. 'He's given me a new drug to try which he thinks a lot of. And he's very keen that I cut certain things out of my diet. He's got an idea that I'm allergic to various food ingredients.'

'Such as?'

She explained everything to him, and the rest of the journey passed in discussing the doctor's theories.

'I've a few jobs to do before we eat, OK?' Brian asked her when they arrived.

'Sure, I'm glad. It'll give me time to prepare the meal.' She wanted to choose her moment to tell him. She hadn't wanted to spring it on him when he was driving the car, or when, still in his working clothes, he was thinking about tidying away implements, and seeing to the animals.

After the meal would be best, or later still, when they took their evening stroll. She was very nervous about it now, afraid he might be angry.

She made the meal as appetising as she knew how. Trying to look as attractive as possible, she changed into a cotton dress of deep blue, scattered with white stars, and matching blue sandals.

'Who's coming to dinner?' Brian teased when he came in, and started removing the worst of the earth from his hands at the kitchen sink.

'You are. Isn't that enough?' she teased.

'Well, just a moment till I make myself smart!' He laughed.

It was one of those warm, lazy summer evenings that go on and on in the Highlands. Even after the sun appears to have set, the sky stays full of light. They'd discovered how pleasant it was to walk up the fields behind the house. From up there they could look back over the tops of the croft buildings, and get quite a fresh aspect. They could hear the muted roar of the stream, hurrying down between their croft and the Campbells' to the sea.

Out beyond lay the sound, an island, and the incredible sunsets that were being put on, night after night, like a special feature show, to delight the eyes.

'Wait till you see the Northern Lights, later in the year,' Brian said as they reached the seat he had set at the best vantage point, before he considered the ground became too steep for Fiona.

Full of suppressed excitement, Fiona decided that this was the right moment.

'Dr Frazer was having a test done for me,' she began slowly.

'A test? What kind of test?'

'Oh, nothing to worry about, love. It's not asthma or anything. As a matter of fact, it's great news! It seems I — or rather we — are going to have a baby.'

Brian went absolutely still. He was so silent for so long, that she stole a glance at him. Had he heard?

'Did you hear what I said?' she asked tentatively.

'Yes. I just can't take it in.'

In fact, Brian's emotions were in turmoil. He wanted a child desperately — but not at any cost. And as Fiona had knowingly defied her doctors' orders and put herself, her life, at risk, who could tell what price they would have to pay?

'See You Soon'

We are all wonderful folk.' Rhona Morrison had appointed herself toastmistress. 'And every now and again we export a young one — a sample — down south, to give them a taste of what we can produce.' She looked round the gathering of Eileen's friends and raised her glass.

'Here's to Eileen!' Her smile was wide and her eyes, through her thick glasses, gleamed with satisfaction.

'Every success, lassie. Every success,' Rhona continued when the murmurs of approval had died down. 'You've got all the ingredients. You're a bonnie lass and a bonnie player.'

Eileen saw the glasses raised to her and felt that none of this was real. Her eyes flickered towards Duncan. He lifted his head and sent her a soul-searching look. Their glances locked for a moment before hers slid away. But he went on staring, steadily and shrewdly, at her. It wasn't just going away that was bothering Eileen. There was something else . . .

'Now, the buffet's ready when you are.'

The toastmistress waved her hand towards the long table at the back of the room, where the waiters were already in attendance to help the guests.

Most of the company, amidst lively chatter, carried their food back to the small tables ranged round the walls.

It is a marvellous party, Eileen instructed herself. Great. The usual fun when everyone else knows everyone so well. Probably I'm the only one here who's not enjoying it.

She saw her father was in buoyant spirits, teasing the life out of Julia. And Julia seemed to glow. They sat nearer the buffet table with Andrew Neilson, the rosy gleam of the wall lights making them look younger.

The hotel was the original village inn; there since the days of the sailing ships, when the recesses of the room would have been in shadow even on a bright summer's day like this.

'Well, what about our plans, then?' Andrew remarked to Willie.

'Ay, Andrew. Ay. I'm glad you like my idea. I'll be down at the yard first thing the morrow's morning.'

'Well.' Andrew's kind face was alight with enthusiasm. 'While you get to work on the old tub I'll be getting on with the new clinker with the lads. Also we've got some repairs to clear. But whenever you're ready, you and I'll get together over the refinements.'

'You mean Willie's actually going to do some work?' Julia said silkily. 'Thank goodness. Maybe that'll stop him moping around wondering what to do with his time. Don't tell me you two are going to turn that old fishing boat in Andrew's yard into a pleasure craft for the visitors!' She intended the remark as a joke, but Willie and Andrew looked comically dismayed.

'Curiosity killed the cat,' Willie taunted. 'I'm not going to let folk who accuse me of lazing around into my secrets.'

'Och well, I'm not all that interested anyway,' said Julia, who was obviously dying to know exactly what was going on.

However, realising Willie wouldn't tell her anything today, she rose hastily on the pretext of going to the cloakroom, and made off, followed by Willie's good-natured chuckle.

Rhona was telling Eileen for the tenth time what pieces to play, how to relax, how not to feel nervous, how she was the greatest wee lassie she'd ever taught, to think well of herself and not to be intimidated.

Eileen kept nodding, but her eyes were curiously glazed.

As she waved goodbye to the group

116

assembled outside the hotel, her habitual air of self-containment aided her, although her mind was wrestling again with the shock phone call.

It was on account of that call that she wasn't taking the train from Inverness or Fort William. She'd arranged to stop over in Glasgow for an hour or two and then to take the sleeper to London.

'Love to Shona when you see her!' someone called.

Eileen smiled non-committally. She was thankful when Duncan let in the clutch. He was driving her to the bus.

His kiss was passionate, yet tender when they said goodbye.

He pressed a little package into her hands and she murmured her thanks distractedly, putting the box in her handbag. They had said their real goodbyes three weeks before.

★ ★ ★

When Eileen alighted from the coach at Buchanan Street Bus Station, she stood for a moment feeling rather forlorn. She hitched up her shoulder-bag. At her feet was a substantial suitcase holding her music as well as her clothes, as she clutched her precious violin case in her hand.

She smiled a little when she remembered her annoyance with Duncan when he'd implied that she might need someone to look after her. Then, to her relief, she realised that there were several taxis lined up close to the bus stance.

She was singularly lucky in her driver. A kind, fatherly, Glasgow man, he took her case from her and listened to her request, and in no time her belongings were safely in the Left Luggage at Central Station and she was on her way, in a state of mounting tension, to the address written on the piece of paper in her hand.

Abstractedly she watched the buildings flow past as the icy knot of anxiety in her stomach got tighter and tighter.

When the taxi drew up in front of the pub in an unimpressive street, her brow furrowed.

'Is this it?' she asked the driver's back.

'The close on the left.' He came out of his cab and round to open the door for her.

She paid him, tipping him generously, and then looked up at the building.

'Good thing we dumped your luggage, eh?' He smiled.

'Yes. Thank you. Thank you for every-thing!'

'No problem.' He gave a genial wave. 'Any time.'

At once her eyes were drawn to Tony's flamboyantly-decorated car parked among the other vehicles at the kerbside. This must be the place.

Nevertheless, when she'd found the right door and pressed the bell, she was thankful that it was Tony himself who appeared.

'Come in,' Tony invited, and Eileen stepped into a rather bleak hallway.

'It's a friend's flat,' he explained. 'We got turfed out of the halls of residence in the summer.' His longish fair hair was rumpled and he wore a slightly distraught expression as he led her towards a doorway. They entered a shabby sitting-room.

'Well, you'd better tell me what all this is about,' she said once they were seated.

'Well, like . . . like I said, it's about Shona. Oh, maybe I shouldn't be saying anything. Maybe it's really none of my business . . . '

'Look, I'm here now, Tony,' Eileen said gently. 'You'd better get it off your chest. On the phone, you said something about Shona 'going off the rails.' What did you mean by that?'

'Well, she's met someone else. He's — he's, well, he's no good, Eileen. Everybody knows that . . . except Shona!'

119

Eileen tried to stay calm, but she felt her spirits sinking.

For his part, Tony seemed relieved to have got the words out. He hunched forward, looking at her earnestly.

'I phoned you because I felt so guilty. After all, Shona wouldn't be in Glasgow if I hadn't talked her into coming. I thought I could keep an eye on her for myself, you see . . . I even decided to stay in the town for the summer to be near her . . . '

Tony's concern for Shona was obviously genuine and Eileen began to wonder if she had misjudged the young man.

'Don't blame yourself.' She stretched out a hand towards him. 'I suppose we should have guessed something like this would happen.' She paused. 'But I thought she was so keen on you!'

'I thought so, too.' Colour deepened his cheeks. 'I thought she was just . . . ' he seemed to dismiss a few simple adjectives, and ended rather lamely with ' . . . great.' He got up and strode to the window. The low sun was getting in his eyes, and he twitched the curtain across with some savagery.

'This guy she's taken up with. None of us have any time for him. But it's all my fault that she met him at the last Union dance before the holidays.' He sat down again, put

120

his head in his hands and stared at the floor. 'He's . . . oh, I don't know how to put it. But none of us would let him near our sisters, if you know what I mean.'

Eileen felt sick. She knew now that Tony wouldn't have brought her here if this wasn't real trouble.

'He dresses like a pop-star — all the latest gear . . . ' He hit the table with his fist. 'He can afford to. And he shows off with that really flashy car of his. He dazzles the girls. But he gets his kicks . . . ' he paused as though he'd just realised something ' . . . *out of sneaking off with other blokes' girlfriends.*'

He stopped abruptly, staring straight ahead, his eyes suddenly veiled, lost in thought.

'I don't know what to say,' Eileen's voice was concerned. 'Opposition, criticism, has always made Shona dig her heels in. I know that sounds lame, but I don't know what to do. I would almost certainly make matters worse if I interfered.'

'I know,' Tony replied. 'Actually, it's great to have someone sensible to discuss this with. You've helped me a lot already, Eileen.' He suddenly straightened and drew his shoulders back. 'Look, have you eaten?'

'N . . . no. It's OK, though. I couldn't eat my lunch for wondering what was the matter with Shona, and now I'm just not hungry.'

'Well, I am now. Would you come to a pizza place with me?'

'Yes. If you'll let me pay.'

'No. I've been making quite a lot of money, fixing up cars for friends . . . It's my sideline. I was saving up to . . . for . . . Oh, well, it doesn't matter now. The point is, I'm loaded.' He laughed, and Eileen suddenly saw the boy who had attracted Shona.

When Tony finally saw her on to the train, however, he didn't look quite so strained and unhappy as when they had first met. At least that was something.

But, when the train finally pulled out, curled up on the top bunk with a prattling female below her, Eileen was assailed by churning thoughts. The farewell at Achnacraig seemed so long ago that it was like a hazy dream.

Fumbling in her handbag, she suddenly came across the little package that Duncan had given her. Her heart gave a small inward tremor of joy as she tore off the wrapping and opened the box.

She wondered what it could be. A brooch perhaps? No. She lifted out a silver chain with three charms hanging on it. The three charms were all rings. She examined them, pondering over Duncan's choice.

One of the tiny rings had a simulated stone in it like an engagement ring. The second was like a wedding ring, and the third in the form of an eternity ring. What had Duncan's thoughts been when he'd chosen her trinket? Had they been bitter, or sentimental?

She began to separate the rings. Mock engagement, mock marriage . . . But — how could you mock eternity?

★ ★ ★

Brian stood for a moment at the top of the high field listening to the strange, sad, musical cry of a curlew. He fancied it was calling, 'Where? Where?' Perhaps it was searching for its mate?

He laughed at himself and looked down over the fields. It was satisfying to see all the fences mended, trim and tight, the result of his own labours. In the field below, the summer grass, green and juicy, was being cropped by several half-grown Angus bullocks. They weren't his. He was grazing them for a farmer. But they looked right there. A sign of things to come — next year.

In a field nearer the road, his potatoes were ready for gathering. some drills were already empty. His planting had been later than his neighbours, but he and Fiona had had their own spuds all July. He could also see his drills of peas and the turnips he had sown. Everything was late this year, of course, but next year would be different.

He'd picked up a lot about crops, fertilisers, protective sprays and so on, but he still had a lot to learn. He and Fiona now enjoyed poring over agricultural magazines in the evenings and discussing their future plans.

Fiona was keen to have ducks and wanted him to contrive a pond in the field beside the burn.

He narrowed his eyes, studying the burn below. He thought he saw a way of channelling off a little stream to flow into a pond he would dig, and then out again and back to the burn.

Eagerly he set off for home, hastening now, to explain his plan to Fiona. He wanted to cheer her up for she didn't seem at all well and he had ordered her to stay in bed.

He found her out at the washing-line hanging up his thick fisherman's jersey.

'I thought I told you not to get up!' he said, concerned.

'I didn't, for a while. And I might go back to bed. I just wanted to get this out. It's such a beautiful day for drying woollens. Sun and breeze. Isn't it lovely?'

'As lovely as you are,' Brian declared.

'Ha, ha! Wait till I get fat!' She laughed.

'You'll just get more beautiful,' he assured her. 'I think I can see how to make a small pond. I wonder if we need anyone's permission to re-direct some of the burn water?'

'Show me! Let's go over to the burn!'

'D'you feel up to it?'

'Oh, I want to. I must see how it would work.'

'Right. Come on. Let's just stroll.'

When he was opening the field gate, he said, 'You know a kid could — a kid who was too wee to go to the shore — could sail a boat on a pond.'

'Yes,' Fiona replied, smiling, thrilled that Brian was already considering such things.

He fastened the gate again.

'D'you know, there's one thing I can't wait to buy for our son. I'm going out to the shop the minute he's born.'

'A christening present! What is it — a silver drinking cup?'

'A pair of wellies!'

Fiona laughed. She couldn't stop laughing. Between coughs she explained that it was the image of a new-born infant wearing wellingtons. She sat down on a stone to recover.

'Maybe you won't have to bother.' She giggled. 'Any son of yours would probably be born wearing them, a fisherman's jersey and a lifeboatman's helmet. Equipped for life in Achnacraig.' She started wheezing.

He left her and ran back to the house for her inhaler. Her condition was really worrying him now.

By the time he returned she was glad of the inhaler and breathed it in gratefully until she was able to thank him.

'Want to go on — or back?'

'On, of course! But not too fast.'

'Lean on me.' His arm encircled her shoulder.

'Now, here's how I'm going to do it.' When they reached the burn, he explained with growing enthusiasm. Encouraged by her joy in the project, he began to embellish his plan, and soon they were day-dreaming about paving, shrubs and a wooden seat.

'Why are you so good to me?' Fiona suddenly interrupted, gazing up at him with wonder in her eyes.

'Because I love you,' Brian replied softly.

'You do everything for me!'

'Look what you're doing for me!' Brian declared. 'Our son will be able to grow up in this wonderful place.'

'Hush, Brian. He might be a girl.' Fiona

126

put a restraining hand on his arm.

'Nonsense. A boy.' He smiled, his eyes twinkling mischievously as he suddenly reached down and scooped her up. 'I'm going to carry you both home,' he told her, but even as he gathered her up into his arms he knew she was too light. Far, far too light. The smile died in his eyes. He mustn't let her know he feared for her — and the baby.

She curled her arms round his neck. 'Brian?'

'Yes?'

'I love you.'

'And I love you. I love you both. I'm holding all my life, everything that's dear to me in my arms.'

Fiona dozed all afternoon, and it was early evening when she heard Brian calling up to her.

'I've brought the jersey in. The wind keeps wrapping it round the rope. Now I'm going to make our meal.'

Fiona sighed contentedly and sank back on the pillows. It was wonderful to be waited on when you felt grotty. Lovely to lie here and not have to make any effort.

After they'd eaten, they played Scrabble while the wind blew louder and louder, gusting round their small, sturdy house.

127

When it grew late, Brian fastened the windows more tightly and drew the curtains.

'Ugh, it's a terrible night. The sea's looking angry. Thank goodness there's no fishing tonight.' He yawned and stretched. 'I'm tired with my day's exertions. You can move over for I'm coming to bed, too.'

When he finally joined her, he stretched out on his back with a contented sigh.

'Best part of the day!'

He sighed again luxuriously.

★ ★ ★

Brian slept deeply but Fiona lay for a while in drowsy contentment, so she was the first to be aware of the bleeper calling.

Her stomach plunged and her heart began to race. This was what she had dreaded ever since Brian had started to train with the lifeboat crew. She looked down at his serene face. He was in such a deep sleep that she wondered for a guilty moment if she could avoid wakening him.

But already he was stirring. Realisation dawned on him. He reached out and switched off the bleeper and in seconds was out of bed and dressing.

Just then Fiona felt the full force of the asthma attack that had been threatening all

128

day. Perhaps the drama of this emergency callout combined with the fearsome weather conditions had been just too much for her.

Even the inhaler, which was lying conveniently by the side of her bed, didn't seem to do anything to ease Fiona's frantic gasping.

Brian's thoughts whirled. What was he to do now? Obviously he was needed on the lifeboat, but how could he leave his wife like this?

Fiona needed help, that was clear. So there was only one thing to do. He'd go down to the harbour as quickly as he could and make sure someone got back to Rowanlea right away to look after her. It would be quicker than trying to get hold of someone by phone.

He caught her in his arms briefly, before he left, explaining what he intended to do.

' 'Bye, darling.' She gasped. 'Take care. See you soon. I — I love you.'

'I'll be two hours at the most.' He guessed, glancing at his watch. It was one o'clock.

Desolation

As Brian drove down the road he could feel the wind buffeting the car. It surely was a wild night. He felt scared inside, not for himself, but for his wife and their unborn child. Fiona looked really ill this time, and he couldn't bear to think how awful the consequences of such a violent attack could be . . .

When he reached the pier, the lifeboat was launched and being held by a rope as the last of the crew got on board. Apparently a yacht had got into difficulties out in the bay, but had managed to send up flares. Brian climbed, in almost one movement, into his gear and jumped on board, cramming his helmet on.

The lights had gone on in most of the village houses when the maroons had gone off, and many of the households would keep vigil until the lads were safely back.

Willie McArthur threw the rope on board and Brian caught it. Relieved to see his old friend, he managed to yell a message to him above the howling gale.

'Willie! Would you send Julia up to the croft to stay with Fiona till I get back? It's urgent — she's not well at all. I'm really worried about her. She'll need the doctor, I think.'

'Right, lad. I'll see to all that. Off you go. Try not to worry about a thing.'

The valiant little boat slewed away from the quay and headed out into the raging darkness.

'Fiona, *dear!*' Julia cried as she let herself into Rowanlea and hurried towards the rigid figure in the armchair.

Fiona was sitting up very straight, her chin lifted and her head back. Her laboured breathing and the wheezing sounds she made filled Julia with apprehension. She shrugged out of her jacket and threw it on a chair near the window, glancing away from the face that was as white as bleached bone, and hunting around in her mind for something comforting to say.

'The doctor's on his way. I asked Willie to make sure. Now just relax. You're not to worry.' Julia stopped when she saw that Fiona was trying to say something. She leaned towards her. 'What's that, dear?' she asked.

'The sea,' Fiona gasped. 'I can't bear the sound of it.' Her grey eyes were fixed anxiously on the window from where the booming and roaring of the sea seemed to enter the room. Intermittently the wind rose and shrieked like a lost soul.

'Well, try not to let it upset you,' Julia advised briskly, coaxing flames to leap in the grate by the liberal use of driftwood. 'I'll make some tea.'

'I couldn't — couldn't drink . . . ' Fiona said huskily and Julia felt another pang of anxiety.

'You'll probably feel like something once I've made it,' she said kindly.

Julia was thankful when Ian Frazer breezed in. Ian was one of those doctors whose very presence brought calmness and confidence.

'Ghastly night,' he declared matter-of-factly, dumping his bag on the table, 'though I've seen worse.' While he was talking he was unpacking a mask and a packet containing capsules.

Julia left him to work over Fiona, went into the kitchen and put the kettle on.

When she came back, carrying a tray, Fiona's distress had been greatly relieved. Having given the girl an injection, the doctor was closing up his bag again.

Fiona managed a wan smile for Julia, who was glad to see that her friend was looking a bit better.

132

The doctor went into the kitchen to dispose of the used syringe and to wash at the sink. He came back to the door drying his hands.

'I'll have to get back down to the harbour in case I'm needed when the boys get back,' he said.

'Drink a cup before you go, Ian. Tea or coffee?' Julia insisted.

'Make it coffee, Julia. Keep me awake!' He turned to his patient. 'Fiona, I'm leaving some capsules with you. And the injection will take effect immediately. It'll relax you.' He took the mug Julia handed him and sipped the coffee gratefully. 'Hm . . . '

He studied Fiona again. 'Relaxation is a good thing for a lady in your condition. I tell you what, Nurse McDonald's a great one for ante-natal relaxation classes. Report to her at the clinic Monday morning at ten o'clock. Right?'

Fiona nodded obediently, faint colour at last creeping into her cheeks.

Julia sent a look half-pitying, half-reproachful towards her and let out an involuntary sigh.

She sighed again after she'd closed the door behind the doctor.

'I was so happy for you when you told me about the baby, dear. But was it wise? That's what I'm wondering. With your asthma, was it wise?'

'I'll manage.' Fiona moved her shoulders in faint defiance. 'How's our campaign to keep the school open coming along, d'you think?' she added, hastily changing the subject.

Glad to have a topic to keep Fiona distracted from the storm and the call-out, Julia plunged eagerly into a summary of all they'd achieved so far.

'I think you were marvellous going round so many of the houses for signatures to the letter of appeal.'

'I've still more calls to make. But I'll need the car . . . ' Fiona stopped to cough.

'Your efforts have wakened up a lot of people and we've had more offers of help with that. So don't worry about it.' Julia's smile of appreciation deepened. 'I'll never forget how angry you were when I told you at first. You'll never know how your fury — and your sympathy — warmed my heart!'

'Well, they got my dander up! Lots more children might appear in the village. Not just Brian's and mine. And it's not just that. It's like chopping off a society at its roots. We've got to fight them!'

Julia chuckled. She remembered how Fiona had amazed her with her sturdy defiance of the authorities; how she'd been immediately active in getting a committee together; and had turned out to be the most imaginative and determined member of it.

If Fiona's health could just match up to her other qualities — she'd be quite a girl!

'I was thinking . . . ' Julia returned to the issue, pumping it for all she was worth in an effort to divert Fiona from the wretchedness she was suffering and to while away the time till Brian would return.

* * *

Down at the harbour and in the village those waiting relaxed when the lifeboat was eventually sighted returning.

Willing hands helped three distressed yachtsmen, one only a boy, to disembark. The boy and one of the men were wrapped in blankets and shivering uncontrollably.

Rory McRory gave Willie a brief summary of what had happened.

The yacht, whose red flare they'd seen, had grounded on a rocky outcrop.

As the lifeboat approached, sending up a parachute flare, they could see that there were three people aboard and that the yacht was being pounded by six or seven-foot waves. Conditions were tricky as the tide was flooding and the wind blowing strongly from the south-west.

The helmsman was about to attempt to bring the lifeboat alongside in the lee of the casualty when a huge wave hit the yacht, rolling her over. As the deck tilted, the young lad, with a yell of fear, went overboard.

Immediately one of the other yachtsmen leaped in after him.

The lifeboat stood by, the men throwing ropes and keeping the searchlight trained on the two figures whom they saw were in difficulty. The boy was panicking and the man seemed to lack the strength needed to deal with him.

'Brian went in,' Rory said proudly. 'With Jock away, he was the strongest swimmer we had. You never saw anything like it! The way he dealt with these two. We got them pulled in. You'll have to hear about it properly later . . .'

'My,' Willie breathed. 'what a blessing he was there. He's a hero, right enough.'

'Ay, he is that. Fearless.'

Willie grasped Brian's hands when he came ashore. He couldn't speak for a moment.

'Lad, I don't know what to say. Just that we're proud to have you here. That you're one of us.' His voice choked. 'Away now and get your wet suit off and hurry along home. I'll phone and tell them you're on your way. We'll have a blether about all the details tomorrow.'

Brian dismissed his thanks with a wave of his hand and disappeared into the shed to change. In no time he was putting the car into gear and turning it away from the harbour.

★ ★ ★

'He's on his way.' Julia had answered the phone at Rowanlea and a relieved smile illuminated her face. 'Thanks, Willie. Thanks for letting us know. Is everyone all right?'

'Well, they've had to leave the yacht to bring the crew ashore. Some of the boys'll be going back out when it gets light. Andrew and the doctor are seeing to the yachtsmen. We've got at least one case of shock and exposure, maybe two.

'But — the main thing is, Julia — they're all safe. And I'm hearing it's all thanks to Brian. He went into the water and got two of them out. All the lads are talking about the courage he showed.' Willie gave a relieved laugh. 'So we can all get back to our beds now, eh, lass?'

'Brian's on his way home, Fiona. He's safe and it seems two men owe their lives to him. Willie's really impressed with the way Brian acted out there — and he's not easily impressed!'

Fiona was almost asleep. A slow, contented smile touched her lips and her eyelids drooped again.

Julia twitched back the curtains to let the maximum light pour out to welcome the returning hero.

'I'll get something hot for him. He won't be ten minutes.'

An hour later Julia turned off the hotplate beneath the soup pan. Something must have delayed Brian. A breath of uneasiness touched her.

Fiona was awake now, her hands gripping the arms of the chair as she fought her old enemy, anxiety. She kept glancing at the clock.

Julia just kept hoping that her friend hadn't really noted the time when Willie had phoned.

It seemed hours later that they heard a car engine and then the crunch of tyres on the gravel.

'Brian!' With a glad cry Fiona stumbled out of her chair and started for the door.

But it was Willie, not Brian, who opened the door and came in, removing his cap as he did so.

At the sight of him something tightened in Fiona's throat.

Willie's face was grey with anguish, his brow beaded with sweat. As he fidgeted uncomfortably with his cap in his hands, Julia became very aware of the ticking of a clock, which was the only sound to break the oppressive silence that filled the room.

'Look, lass, you'd better sit yourself down,' Willie said at last. 'There's been an accident. And it was nothing to do with the sea.'

'It — it's not Brian, is it?' Fiona whispered.

'I'm afraid so. It was the car . . . He was obviously hurrying to get home to you. He must have been going too fast, and he was probably worn out. Anyway, he lost control of the car and it went over the cliff.' Willie's eyes misted with tears. 'I'm sorry, Fiona.'

'You mean, he — he's . . . ?'

'Ay, lass, he's gone.' Now that he'd said it, Willie slumped into the chair opposite the young girl, who remained strangely in control, despite her deathly pallor.

'I don't know what to say to you,' he choked out. 'I just don't have the words. But Brian was the very son I would like to have had. I loved him, too, Fiona.' He wiped the salty tears from his eyes with the back of his workworn hand. 'He'd just saved two men out of the sea. It's terrible, terrible.'

Fiona seemed strangely isolated from the other two. Her face was etched with stunned disbelief.

'He was hurrying home to you, lass,' Willie went on. 'But he wouldn't have been away at all if I hadn't asked him to go on the lifeboat. Now he's gone, and . . . it's all my blame.'

'No, it's not your fault,' Fiona replied gently. 'Brian wanted to do it. He was always keen to be out with the others on the boats . . .' Suddenly a fine tremor began to shake her body. It increased until she was shuddering violently, while her huge eyes mutely begged them to tell her it wasn't true, that there had been some ghastly mistake . . .

Perhaps Brian wasn't dead at all. Perhaps he would come back to her again. Perhaps . . .

And so Agnes Campbell found them when she opened the back door quietly and came in carrying a basket with food and drink in it. It was she who fetched a rug and wrapped it round Fiona and went and filled a kettle for a hot-water bottle for her to hold.

Willie was obviously grief stricken, but somehow managing to hang on to his dignity. Julia's eyes were wet with tears.

But it was Fiona who had the most profound effect on Agnes. Looking sorrowfully at her young neighbour, Agnes thought she had never seen such desolation on a face.

★ ★ ★

Shona's eyes sparkled. Excitement and pleasure always had that effect on her, and she was both excited and very pleased with life. The customer she was serving thought it was a long time since she'd met such a happy, friendly salesgirl.

Shona was selling cosmetics, but she was also a trainee beauty consultant. She thought she must be about the luckiest girl in the world. She'd been chosen from a number of girls for this super job and — she'd been chosen by Charles Ogilvie to be his girlfriend!

As the customer moved away Shona's heart did a triple somersault. She'd just caught sight of her new boyfriend wandering round the department. He caught her eye, sending her an amorous look that caused the colour in her cheeks to deepen.

Charles had come to meet her. It was almost closing time. Soon they would be zipping out into the country in his beautiful car.

The car, which actually belonged to his firm, was a two-litre saloon and very powerful. The city seemed to be left behind in a flash. Their destination was a small, lochside hotel.

The dining room, when they entered it, was warm and mellow with a rich scent and soft, rosy lighting. The food was good, their conversation desultory now.

Shona had a drowsy sense of anticipation while she ate and drank and felt more headily attracted to her handsome companion. She went into the cloakroom before they left. She stared at herself in the mirror and then looked hastily away. She didn't want to confront herself. She didn't want to think. She only wanted to drift with the current.

During the drive back she fell asleep. She had felt so drowsy. The cocktail had been a very large one, the wine had been poured liberally, although Charles himself had only one glass.

'This isn't my flat,' she murmured sleepily, looking out of the car window when Charles brought it to a halt.

'No. It's mine. You're coming in for a cup of coffee to wake you up before you face your flatmates. You're a little bit tipsy.'

'I am not!' she contradicted him but was glad of his steadying hand when she got out of the car. 'Mind you, I probably shouldn't have had that last glass of wine.'

But as soon as the door was closed behind them, he caught her in his arms.

'I couldn't wait for this,' he murmured, so exactly echoing her thoughts that she pulled him even closer. 'I don't want to leave you to make the coffee, Shona.'

'Well, we can make it later, can't we?'

'Mmm . . . '

Her thoughts blurred and melted as he lifted her and carried her through to his bedroom. He laid her, like a rag doll, on the bed and began to kiss her with a renewed intensity.

She responded eagerly. She must be mad. She'd never behaved like this with anyone before. But if this was madness it was glorious.

She raised her hand to caress his hair and, in so doing she accidentally swept something to the floor from the bedside cabinet.

'Whoops!' Charles lay across her to trail his fingers in the carpet in pursuit of the object and brought up a tiny, gold earring.

'Were your earrings hurting you, darling?' His voice was soft with endearment.

'My earrings? But I wasn't wearing any!'

'Oh, I thought . . . OK. Never mind. They must be my mum's. She was visiting me last weekend.' He nuzzled her neck and she could feel the passion welling up inside her as she responded with an intensity that almost frightened her. No man had ever had the power to rouse her so.

Just then the telephone shrilled. Charles groaned.

'I'm not going to answer that!' Then, 'Oh, well, I suppose I'd better or it'll go on ringing all night.'

In spite of his reluctance, he closed the door very carefully behind him. He didn't return immediately as she'd expected. Although she couldn't hear his words, he seemed to be engaged in a lengthy argument.

Mischievously, headily, she thought it would be fun to creep out and join him — entwine herself round him and tease him as he phoned. She would go silently and surprise him.

She crossed the room on tiptoe and carefully began to open the door. And there she froze. She could hear his words very clearly.

'But, Sylvia, darling, I *do* love you. I just couldn't help this business dinner tonight. *I must go now.* The chap's waiting for me. We'll meet as usual tomorrow.'

The last words Shona heard as she turned away were, 'Sure, I'll bring your earrings . . . '

A steely glint kindled in Shona's eyes. Fury

144

and disgust catapulted her across the room, feeling as though she'd been doused with icy water.

She was pushing her feet into her shoes when Charles reappeared.

'You beast!' She gasped at him, her furious face telling him that she had overheard.

'All right, all right,' he blustered, 'so you're not the only girl in my life. Why should you be?' He caught at her as she brushed past him. 'Not so fast! You're not going — you little tease!'

Displaying strength and speed she didn't know she had, she whirled away and reached the hall.

Charles charged after her. 'Come back, you little so and so — you haven't paid for that expensive dinner yet!'

Sick with fury and self-disgust, Shona flew from him. His flat door crashed shut behind her retreating figure.

★ ★ ★

Shona sobbed as she ran, and kept on running until she reached a familiar street. Then still sobbing and rubbing her tear-stained cheeks, she eventually gained her own close. Thoroughly exhausted now, she dragged herself up the long flights of stairs

145

with the aid of the hand rails.

Luckily her flatmates were still out. She hurried into the bathroom and turned on the bath taps. She felt contaminated — and utterly humiliated. She wanted to scrub and scrub and make herself clean again.

Oh, how could she have been such a naive fool? Her confidence was gone. She just wanted to hide for the rest of her life. What was life anyway? Just a snare. A trap.

It was the turn of her telephone to shrill as she was going wearily to bed. Her first thought was to ignore it. She thought if it was her father she might burst into tears. Finally she lifted the receiver and gave the number in a small, tired voice.

'Shona? It's Eileen! Are you all right. You sound . . . '

'Oh, Eileen . . . ' It was all Shona could manage. Tears blurred her voice.

'Shona, Shona! Don't cry. What's the matter, pet? Have you heard then?'

'H . . . heard?'

'Dad's been trying to get you. Where have you been?'

'I — I went out — straight from work.'

'Brian Hamilton's been killed.'

For a moment there was silence on the phone as Shona tried to take in the terrible words.

146

'B — Brian? He can't have. I don't believe it.' Shona's legs turned to rubber and she sat down hurriedly. 'Not Brian, Eileen?' she pleaded, her voice trembling. 'Oh, not Brian?'

Eileen couldn't speak for a moment or two. And then she said, 'Dad's shattered. Brian's car went over a cliff.'

Shona's small fist beat the phone table repeatedly, but she didn't feel the pain.

'Blast the car! Blast the cliffs! Blast everything!' Tears ran down her cheeks and her voice choked.

Eileen tried hard not to break down herself.

'Poor Fiona. It's dreadful. She's so delicate, too,' she said, trying to keep her own voice steady.

'Yes.' Shona gave a gulp. 'Poor *Fionna*.' She used the warm Gaelic version of the name, with a strange new sense of her own heart growing larger and capable of embracing someone else's pain.

The line went silent again for a while as neither of them could speak.

It was Eileen who once more made the effort.

'Shona.' She took a deep breath. 'Before I told you, you were already upset . . . What's wrong?'

Shona took a deep breath to steady her voice.

'It was a man. I've been so stupid, Eileen. I thought he was in love with me! I've made a complete, utter, unbelievable fool of myself. But it doesn't matter now . . . '

'Oh, Shona!'

'It's all right. Nothing dreadful happened. I just found out in time that my magic dream was just a . . . was just a one-night adventure for him.' She drew in a gasp of air.

'Oh, Shona, I'm sorry!' Eileen exclaimed. 'Will you be all right?'

'Yes, I'll . . . Yes, the others will be in soon. I'll wait up for them.'

'Good night, darling,' Eileen said fondly. 'Take care.'

A Glimmer Of Hope

Goodbye, dear.' Brian's mother kissed Fiona tearfully. 'Now, remember, come and stay with us before the birth, or after. It's all the same. We'll be good to you . . . for Brian's sake.' She wiped her red eyes with an already soaking handkerchief.

' 'Bye, Fiona!' Brian's sister embraced her. 'Come soon. Come and have the baby in Glasgow. The Queen Mother's a marvellous hospital! Maybe it'll be a wee boy — and we can call him Brian . . . ' Her voice cracked and she rasped in a breath.

Fiona's own aunt was busily stacking plates and putting glasses on a tray in a fussy, anxious way.

As though she couldn't have waited till the Hamilton family had gone, Fiona thought tiredly.

The Hamiltons climbed into their two cars, lamenting the fact that most of them had jobs and had only been given a few days' compassionate leave for the funeral.

'Now, remember!' Mrs Hamilton called, winding down the window as they drove away. 'Come to Glasgow soon, dear. We'll

manage somehow. Billy can go and stay at
Betty's and you can have his room.' Her
voice tailed away as the car gained speed.
'As soon as you've sold the house . . . '

Julia turned from waving them off and
took a startled look at Fiona. She'd been
pale before, but now she was a yellowish-grey
colour and looked ready to faint.

'Fiona!' She hurried over to her friend and
took her arm. 'Are you all right?'

'No! Not really, Julia. You'll have to get
the doctor for me — quickly. Could you?'

'Come,' Julia supported her. 'Lie down
first and then I'll phone him.'

'Yes, yes, dear.' Fiona's aunt bustled over.
'I don't think you're very well, dear, are you?
Now, I'll help you. Into bed. Into our bed in
the downstairs room.

'Oh dear! Oh dear! What'll we do? What'll
we do?' She sucked in her breath several
times in utter consternation.

Fiona rolled her eyes towards her aunt and
whispered a 'Dear heavens,' that only Julia
could hear.

Julia hurried to the phone while Aunt Ethel
heaped the downie haphazardly over Fiona.

Fiona's head fell back as she tried to
breathe deeply and slowly. Slowly and
deeply. Slowly and deeply, she told herself.
I must not, must not, lose Brian's baby. The

refrain kept going over and over in her brain as, clammy with weakness and nausea, she sensed that her heart's desire was breaking away from her.

She slipped out of consciousness for a few moments, to the accompaniment of Aunt Ethel's gasped anxieties. And it seemed to her that almost immediately, Dr Frazer was sitting on the side of the bed, holding her wrist and calming her.

'Now, now. It's probably nothing to worry about — just a reaction to all the strain.' His words were balm to her sore spirit. 'You're going to sleep now. Just a small jag . . . There! You'll have a lovely . . . peaceful . . . sleep. And your baby will be all right. Do you hear me? It — will — be — all — right.'

He was different with Julia.

'I said that to calm her.' He rubbed his damp brow. 'I'll have to get her to hospital in Inverness but how on earth will she stand the journey?' He looked at Julia fiercely as though she could provide a professional opinion for him.

'Well?' he asked distractedly of everyone there.

'I could drive her.' Willie stepped forward. 'Though she'd be better off in an ambulance.'

Fiona's uncle, silver haired and worried,

stood by the window looking anguished, lifting his hands helplessly.

'Don't move her! Don't move her!' His wife fluttered nervously. 'Moving her would be dangerous, dangerous! She's got to lie flat.'

Ian Frazer looked at her with ill-concealed impatience.

He raised his hand to calm her.

'OK, OK, don't worry. I think it's probably best if we let her lie still just now.'

Julia walked out to the doctor's car with him.

'I think she'll lose the baby,' he told her bluntly, his face dark with the sympathy he obviously felt for his patient.

Julia laced her fingers together in despair. Oh, no! Not the baby. Not after Brian! Her heart bled for Fiona. And Willie? What would he do? He would blame himself for this, too . . .

Dr Frazer looked anxiously down at his watch. He should be getting back to his surgery.

'Look, Julia.' He put a reassuring hand on her shoulder. 'I've done all I can for Fiona meantime. The best thing now is for her to rest, but if there are any more problems just give me a ring.'

Julia gave him a worried smile. 'I'll have to

go soon myself. I've got so much preparation for the school opening after the summer holidays that I can't put it off any longer. But I'll let Fiona's aunt know the situation.'

'Her aunt, yes . . . well.' The doctor sighed heavily. 'Frankly I think she's liable to do more harm than good, but just now we've no choice. I'll call back to see Fiona as soon as I possibly can,' he told her as he got into his car.

★ ★ ★

Only when Julia had satisfied herself that Fiona was settled and asleep, would she let Willie drive her back to the village.

'It was good of Shona to come up for the funeral,' she remarked, trying to sound cool as she fastened her seat-belt.

Willie reversed the car around the side of the house. 'Just like her. She was very distressed. Eileen wanted to come. She would have been there, too, if she could have managed it.'

'How's she getting on?' Julia enquired.

'Very well.' Willie changed down to turn on to the shore road. 'We'll see her in the concert halls yet.'

'What did she play for the maestro?'

'She says she had to play a movement from

a Mozart concerto to be tested for musicality — and she got praised for that.'

'That must be something!' Julia exclaimed.

'Mmm! And a couple of Paganini caprices for virtuosity,' Willie informed her, every inch the proud father.

'I wonder how that went?'

'I think it went fine. She said something about Bach and Fritz Kreisler. She's a rare one — isn't she? Our Eileen?' Willie paused while he negotiated his way round a slow-moving tractor. 'My, but I miss her! I miss them both, so much. Still, it's a relief to know Shona's managed to find a job she likes. But she'll always be my wee girl.'

Julia smiled. There could be no fonder father than Willie McArthur, she thought to herself.

'There you are now, Julia.' He pulled up at the schoolhouse gate. 'Will you be going back to Rowanlea later? I'll maybe come for the stroll. Give me a shout when you're ready to leave.'

* * *

The doctor's car was outside Rowanlea when Julia and Willie approached it in the evening.

Aunt Ethel let them in. 'It's terrible, terrible.' She was wringing her hands.

154

'Fiona's so poorly, it's such a worry, I just . . . '

Julia was hardly listening as she began to hasten through to her friend.

'No, no!' Aunt Ethel detained her with a sharp grip on her arm.

Julia looked down at the little hand. Aunt Ethel was like a little, pecking bird, for ever nodding and repeating herself, yet that was a determined little claw on her arm. And it stayed there until Julia shrugged and turned back to the living-room.

After about ten minutes Dr Frazer put his head round the door and asked if Fiona's uncle would come and have a word with him.

Hugh Burroughs rose with alacrity and went out with the doctor. They strolled the verge of the lawn as they talked.

Ian Frazer was curt. 'Your wife's not doing Fiona any good over-reacting to everything the way she does. She's making Fiona agitated, which is the worst thing for her!'

'I feared as much.' Uncle Hugh groaned softly.

'I'm thinking the best chance,' the doctor went on, 'is to keep Fiona here. Bed rest — twenty-four hours a day.'

'I see.' Fiona's uncle sighed. 'It'd be better if we left. Wouldn't it?' They reached the hedge, turned and retraced their footsteps. 'But I hate the thought of abandoning her at this time.'

He stopped and looked along towards the village.

'How would it do . . . ' He spoke hesitantly. 'If we — if we stayed in bed and breakfast? I saw a bed and breakfast sign outside a nice grey stone house down there. D'you think if Ethel and I moved there? Then we'd be on hand . . . ?'

The doctor's eyes lit up. 'You'd be well looked after there. And I think it's a first-class idea. Good for you!' He took the other man by the arm. 'Now, let's go in and have a word with the others.'

'So, who's going to look after Fiona?' the doctor pondered, after the new plan had been explained.

Aunt Ethel, far from complaining about having to move, had looked silently relieved.

'We'll come up every day, every day,' she promised earnestly.

'I'm taking a gamble,' Ian Frazer continued, 'but I think this way there's the least risk. She stays in bed till I say she can get up. We need a quiet, friendly, yet efficient person to stay with her.'

'I'll stay,' Julie said. 'You must see. It has to be me.'

156

In the silence that followed they all looked at her; the two Burroughs with relieved gratitude, the doctor thoughtfully — and Willie with consternation.

'But the school starts next week!' he exclaimed. 'And who'll run the school?'

Julia faced him. 'The person who ran it when I had that bad virus — Andrew Neilson!'

'And who'll look after Andrew's yard?' he asked, still unconvinced.

'You!'

A look of surprised interest came into Willie's eyes.

'If Andrew Neilson has a boatyard, how can he be a teacher?' Uncle Hugh wanted to know.

'He's teacher trained and has a degree,' Julia told him. 'He decided against teaching as a career. But, in fact, he's a rare teacher — when he wants to be.'

'Do you think he would do it?' Ian Frazer queried.

Julia spread her hands, and smiled. 'We can only ask him.'

'No time like the present. Let's you and me and Willie go in my car and see Andrew now!'

★ ★ ★

157

Andrew Neilson could hardly hold back a grin when he rang the handbell and the children lined up in front of him at the school door. Rôle-playing with a vengeance, he thought wryly to himself. Fancy letting Julia talk him into this!

One reason for his agreeing, he knew, was a swift sympathy for the plight of Fiona Hamilton. His heart bled for her. He wanted to do something to help. He'd already been in touch with his bosses regarding financial assistance for her from the Mission Fund.

The children were well behaved, rather too quiet, he thought, as though sensing an emergency. They were also unused to their temporary teacher and not sure how far they could go with him.

As the school-day wore on, Andrew got into the swing of things and decided to indulge himself for the last half-hour by devoting it to nature study. He dived into his favourite subject of local bird visitors, and was astounded by the amount of information he received from the pupils.

Here was a source of observation and knowledge he'd previously discounted when they'd started the local bird book, although Julia was always on about harnessing the children's skills. Suddenly, to his astonishment, Andrew found he was enjoying himself.

And to think he was the one who had set himself against the campaign to keep the village school open. Well, he'd certainly changed his mind now.

For the last few minutes he settled the children to colouring in photo-copies of one of the waders and proceeded to tidy up the schoolroom with a view to making the school cleaner's job easier.

As he worked he thought of the night Fiona Hamilton had come, eager eyed, to his house, to get his signature for the appeal to keep the school open.

'But I don't agree!' he'd told her, and saw the light fade from her eyes to be replaced by a puzzled, half-laughing reproof.

'You're teasing me,' she'd said in disbelief.

'No. Really. It's got to be more economically viable to bus the children — and have them all taught in a bigger school.'

'Economically!' she exclaimed scornfully. 'Who's talking about economics! We're talking about a vibrant community — a way of life — a culture . . . ' She ran out of breath.

'Oh, come now . . . ' The argument had escalated and his eyes gleamed at the memory of the cut and thrust of it.

'Please, sir?'

'Yes, Mhairi?'

159

'Please, sir. It's four o'clock.'

'Oh! So it is. Sorry! You can clear up now.'

He rubbed his hand down over his face when they'd all scampered away. It hadn't gone too badly. Maybe they'd remember something. They were good kids, well disciplined, polite and sensible — and by George, they knew about the local wildlife! They were, after all, the Achnacraig folk of tomorrow.

Maybe Fiona Hamilton's arguments weren't so far out!

There was still plenty of time to go down to the yard and see how the lads were getting on.

When Andrew arrived there, Willie was busy removing paint from the old fishing boat they were going to convert into a pleasure craft.

Three weeks later, Andrew was still teaching and Willie had made a lot of progress in making the hull watertight.

'How's it going, Willie?' Andrew had arrived after school finished on Friday.

'Fine. Fine! And how's the teaching going?'

'All right, I think. But I wonder how much longer? How are things at Rowanlea?'

'Fiona's still confined to bed. I'll say one

160

thing, though, that girl's got a lot of guts. Julia says she's quite determined not to lose Brian's baby.'

'Yes,' agreed Andrew thoughtfully, 'you can't really help but admire her.'

'I'm taking a wander up there this evening,' Willie went on.

'Tell Julia I must see her about the monthly tests. Och, never mind, I'll be going up myself to see Fiona about the Mission Fund,' Andrew said, then his attention was taken up by the boat.

'Willie, there's too much rotten wood on that old wheelhouse to make it worth repairing. Pick it down when you're ready. I'm going to build a whole new one. I'll build it in the shed. Here's the plan I've made.' He took a folded piece of paper out of his inside pocket. 'As soon as this teaching's over,' he added.

* * *

It wasn't the first time Willie had been at Rowanlea since Julia had moved in. He'd been up every day, doing a lot of the outside work and almost always bringing something with him to give comfort or pleasure. Tonight he'd cut some roses from his garden and carried them carefully.

161

'They're lovely, Willie!' Julia took them at the door with a smile of appreciation. 'Mmm. What a lovely perfume!'

'They're for you,' Willie said deliberately, looking into her eyes and thinking that they looked shadowed.

'Not for Fiona?' she asked, surprised.

'Not this time. They're for the nurse.'

'You're nice, Willie.'

'Away with you,' he admonished, his colour deepening.

'Come in. We'll have a strupack?' Julia invited.

'Not yet. I'll take a look out the back and see that everything's in order.'

'Willie McArthur, are you thinking that I wouldn't have fed the hens or something?'

'Ach, I could have done that for you, Julia. I'm thinking you're doing too much.'

'Away with you, too, then. That's nonsense. I have to look after her. I have to do it, Willie.'

'I know,' he grunted, 'but I still feel it's too much. You're going to make yourself ill, what with looking after Fiona nearly twenty-four hours a day, seeing to your own affairs and still keeping in touch with the school. I'm sure Fiona wouldn't want you to overdo things.'

Julia smiled to herself — Willie's concern

162

was really quite touching.

'Listen, Willie,' she said softly. 'I'm OK, honestly I am. I haven't anything to think about except Fiona, now that the school is definitely in Andrew's capable hands. It was such a relief when the authorities agreed to let him take temporary responsibility.'

Willie looked at her thoughtfully.

'Well, don't hesitate to ask if you need me. You know I'm always there.' Then, before she could reply, he'd swiftly moved past her and out the back door.

Julia put the flowers in a vase and then sat down and regarded them, only her eyes kept closing. The heavy rose-perfume spread all around her. Despite what she'd told Willie, she did feel very tired. This was silly. She forced open her eyes. She must let Fiona smell them, too. She got up and carried the vase through to the other room.

She'd left Fiona reading, but now the book lay, cover up, on the bed. Fiona had fallen into a little nap, her pretty mouth drooping sadly at the corners.

Julia placed the flowers on the table and sat down on the chair by the bed. Her own eyelids were again growing very, very heavy. Poor Fiona, she thought, poor pet. Life could be very cruel.

When Willie came in from the back after

an hour, he put his head round the door and took in the scene.

'Two sleeping beauties!' he exclaimed, rousing Julia, who blinked at him as though coming back from far away.

It seemed the most natural thing in the world to go and kneel beside her, and put his arms round her; quite natural, too, for Julia to sink tiredly into those arms.

'Julia, you're going to crack if you don't take a rest — '

Julia didn't answer. The moment was too sweet. She was overwhelmed by a deep, deep love.

Willie's heart burned with the pure joy of holding her. His eyes began to shine, and then to mist over with the warmth of his emotion. No more words were necessary. Indeed, words might spoil the ecstasy. But the silence was packed with warm communication. The ecstasy might be all too brief.

Fiona's eyes fluttered open and she saw, for the first time, her two friends very close together and, perhaps they didn't know it, so in love. Some light seemed to come into Fiona's life, together with a glimmer of hope. Her drooping mouth straightened and then curved up at the corners. She raised herself on her elbows and regarded them and a spark of warmth crept into her eyes.

And then she smiled. A wide, generous, loving smile lit up her face, like the sun bursting out from cloudshreds. It was the first time she'd smiled since Brian had died and it was the first time since then that she'd really felt like smiling.

Julia had never seen a smile so beautiful.

'How about a strupaok, then?' Julia suggested.

'That would be lovely,' Fiona said warmly.

'Well, I'll make it.'

'No, I will,' Willie insisted. 'I've already put the kettle on.'

'Both make it.' Fiona looked at them with affection, sinking back on her pillows. 'Both make it and take all the time in the world. There's no hurry.'

Her smile lingered when they'd gone. Her thoughts were no longer inturned to the grief she felt, or her worries about the baby. Instead she was thinking about her two dear friends — obviously quite hopelessly in love. Julia and Willie . . . Well!

Making Progress

It won't be easy. But we've got to do it. I've quite made up my mind, Hugh. We must do it. We must offer Fiona and the baby a home. We can't abandon them, or let the Hamiltons have them. Will we go and tell her now?'

Hugh Burroughs laughed shortly. 'Yes. But just a minute, Ethel. There are a few more things we must work out . . .'

They were still earnestly discussing the arrangements and changes they would have to make to accommodate Fiona and the baby, when they reached Rowanlea.

Nurse MacDonald's car was at the door so they knew that Fiona would be practising her relaxation exercises under the nurse's directions.

'They won't be long,' Julia told them. 'I've just put the kettle on for Nurse's tea.' She led them into the living-room.

'She'll be through in a minute,' she went on. 'Can you smell my baking? You're just in time! Oh, and I hear more footsteps. We're going to have a ceilidh!' She opened the back door to find Duncan there scraping his boots.

'Easier to take them off, Duncan!' Julia suggested brightly.

'Ay! Right enough.' He came in in his stocking-soles. 'That's the bottom field ready now, Julia.'

'That's great, Duncan. Good for you! Fiona will be grateful. Sit down. The tea's just coming.'

'What are you up to these days, Duncan?' Hugh Burroughs settled back in his seat when the greetings were over.

'All sorts of things. There's plenty to do on the crofts at the back end. And there's work on the boat. Ay — and a few entertainments.' Duncan grinned mischievously. 'I was at a dance over at Lochend last night.'

'Huh! Still gallivanting all over the country-side, Duncan Campbell! Are you never going to settle down?' Julia had come through with the tray.

'Julia! I'm only a lad!' His soft words belied the look of irritation he shot her making Julia feel strangely uneasy. It seemed to her to say — Who persuaded my love to go away? And are you now telling me I have to pine quietly at home? Well, I've no intention of doing that!

The moment passed when the tea was handed round and he began to make polite conversation with the Burroughses.

'Heard from Eileen?' Julia asked, as she handed him the pancakes.

'She's been offered a place in a three-year course in the College of Music,' Duncan informed her.

Julia whirled. Willie hadn't told her that!

'D'you think she'll take it?' she asked, unable to contain her excitement.

'Ay.' His gaze challenged her again. 'I expect she'll take it!' he said coldly.

Unflinching, she met the hard accusation in his eyes before she heard the welcome distraction of Nurse MacDonald coming through from the other room.

'Here's your tea, Nurse. And a ceilidh provided!' Julia forced gaiety into her voice and managed to produce what sounded like a cheerful laugh for the company's benefit. 'Now tell us all how Fiona is progressing?'

* * *

Nurse MacDonald settled down, pleasantly accepting the limelight. 'Och, I'm very happy with her relaxation technique. Very happy. She's practising it on her own, too, and oh — what a difference! She's a model mum-to-be!'

'D'you think she'll be able to get up soon?'

'For spells, yes. She's about ready for that. She's done very well.'

'Is that Fiona's tea you're pouring, Julia?' Aunt Ethel rose and put her cup on the table. 'I'll take it through. Hugh and I want to see her.'

'Och.' Nurse MacDonald rose suddenly, making up her mind. 'Fiona's missing all the fun. She can come through in her robe for a few minutes. It'll do her good. I'll fetch her.'

Aunt Ethel set down the cup again and her fingers made staccato taps against the table while her husband moved uneasily.

'Hello, dear!' they chorused warmly when their niece appeared.

'Hi, Fiona,' Duncan greeted her with a lazy salute and helped himself to another pancake.

Fiona sat down and glanced about her with pleasure in her eyes.

'This is nice,' she said. 'How is everyone?'

'We're all a lot happier for seeing you looking perkier!' her uncle told her.

'We've come to see you,' her aunt put in hastily. 'We've got a lovely surprise and we've quite made up our minds!'

Fiona's eyes widened and she opened her mouth to speak.

'Wait!' Her aunt waved her hand. 'Don't

say anything. It's all arranged. Isn't it, Hugh?' Her voice rose and trembled a little as she made her announcement. 'You are coming home to stay with us in the borders!'

In the silence that followed Ethel took out a wisp of handkerchief and dabbed at her eyes, and a faint scent of lavender wafted across the room.

The silence grew as they waited for Fiona to speak.

'No, Aunt Ethel,' she said slowly and decisively. 'I'm staying here!'

Aunt Ethel looked at her husband as if for support.

Hugh Burroughs was too surprised to help her out.

Into the stunned silence that followed, her aunt's small, fluttery voice wavered again.

'S . . . Staying here?'

'Yes, Aunt Ethel, thank you. Thank you for asking me. But, yes, I'm staying here,' Fiona told her resolutely. 'This is where Brian wants — wanted — his son to be . . . brought up. And this is where we shall stay.'

★ ★ ★

Shona was dreaming that she was walking on the shore with Tony and that happiness

170

enfolded them. Then she woke up and the familiar, heavy, uneasy feeling was sliding between the dream and reality.

What was the matter, again? Oh, yes! She'd messed up her friendship with Tony.

The day ahead was empty and grey. There was only work and the companionship of her flat-mates in the evening. She'd had no desire to accept any invitations from other male friends.

Wearily she dragged herself from bed and began automatically to shower and dress and put on her make-up. To all outward appearances when she was finished she looked a well-groomed, successful, young woman hurrying to a satisfying job.

In fact she looked more than that. She looked quite stunningly beautiful. She wore a geranium-pink suit with matching shoes and her blouse was a dazzling white. Her hair no longer swirled and tumbled but was perfectly shaped to enhance the fine bones of her face. With the shadows carefully concealed and a hint of blue shading, her eyes looked huge and luminous.

They were the first thing Tony noticed as he nearly crashed into her as he hurried up Byres Road. His face went white and for a moment broke into an expression of anger.

Shona's heart turned right over then she

171

felt the colour rushing to her cheeks.

Both were confused.

'I'm heading for the subway . . .' she stated inanely.

'Oh?' His voice was icy. 'I'm on my way to work on a car, hence the gear.' He was wearing a boiler suit. His hair was tumbled and she felt an almost irresistible urge to reach up and lift some strands from his forehead.

'Where?' she asked, to play for time.

'At Maryhill. Micky's loaned me his garage.'

'Oh!' An expression of strain crossed her face. She couldn't think of anything else to say. And he seemed so cold and angry.

'You'll be late if you don't hurry!' he suggested.

'Yes.' She ought to move away, but her legs seemed to have turned to water.

They both moved in the same direction and collided. He had to catch her arm to prevent her from toppling over. Her heart was beating so fast now that she was sure he must hear it. She tore herself away from him and began to run towards the subway, whirling round briefly at the entrance, hoping to catch a last glimpse of him, but he was a block away, striding purposefully up the road.

A moment later he suddenly stopped and put his foot on a low sill to retie a perfectly-knotted shoelace. He slid his eyes to the right to try to catch a glimpse of a pink suit — but it had already vanished from sight.

Shona swayed in the subway, choking back threatening tears. All she wanted was to be alone somewhere, where she could weep and weep, and try to wash away all the pain of loving Tony.

She stumbled up the steps at St Enoch's. Somehow she must pull herself together and get through the day as best she could.

* * *

A week passed. A week in which Shona learned anew that it was possible to go on from day to day with her heart broken. There was no joy in living, only a certain grim satisfaction in knowing you could put up a good front and nobody need know that your life was in ruins. Only the girls in the flat knew how unhappy Shona was, and they were kind and sympathetic.

'There's a message for you, Shona,' Vivien told her cheerfully, when Shona came in from work on Saturday evening. 'It was lying on the mat. I've put it on the phone table.'

Shona lifted the unstamped envelope wonderingly. There was a faint oily smudge on it.

Her heart leaped as she tore open the note. There was just a few lines on a large sheet of paper.

Meet me at the Cul de Sac tomorrow at seven, she read. *We've got to talk. If you don't come, I'll understand. Tony.*

She began to cry and the tears splashed on the letter in her hand.

'What's the matter?' Vivien came and put an arm round her. 'Not bad news, is it?'

'N . . . no,' Shona stuttered. 'At least, I don't know. It's from Tony. He wants to talk. D'you think? Oh, Viv, I'm so scared!'

★ ★ ★

It was a warm September day and Fiona sat at the living-room window sewing, and occasionally resting her eyes by looking out of the window.

Grief was a funny thing. You could go on for a while not feeling anything much, maybe if you were reading a book or talking to someone. And then suddenly, you lifted your head and looked out at the border he'd planted, or the gravel he'd brought up from the shore — and it was there again

174

threatening to engulf you.

A tear brimmed over and dropped on to the little garment in her hands and her fingers grew still because she could no longer see her own tiny stitches.

Blinking back the tears, she tried to focus her eyes on the shore road. She laid her work down. There was also this terrible weariness which made even the smallest task seem like a marathon.

Then she could see Agnes Campbell coming along from the village. Good! She'd be coming in to see them. She was bringing them morning rolls from the village shop, the daily paper and a carton of milk.

'Here's Agnes!' she called to Julia, who was out in the kitchen.

'Right, I'll get the strupak!' Julia called cheerfully.

Agnes strode up the path with the energy of a much younger person, opened the front door after the token knock, and came in like a fresh breeze.

'My, it's good to see you up, Fiona. You're doing fine, are you?'

'Yes. Fine,' Fiona assured her, smiling.

'Grand. Grand!' Agnes exclaimed.

' 'Morning, Julia. How's the strupak?' Agnes called through to the kitchen, where she could hear Julia busying about.

'Coming!' Julia called back.

They sat round the window-table with their tea. Agnes obviously had something on her mind and was just waiting till they were all settled to express it.

'Julia. Now that Fiona's getting up, it's time you were returning to your work!'

'I know. I'll have to get back, Agnes.' A small frown formed between Julia's eyes. 'But I don't think Fiona's quite ready to be left on her own yet.'

'It need only be for the hours you're away.' Agnes's firm brown face was kind. 'I'll come in both morning and afternoon. And I won't let you down.'

Julia's face cleared. She turned questioningly to Fiona, who put her hand on her friend's arm.

'You've been wonderful to me, Julia. You must get back.' She turned to her neighbour. 'I've been trying to persuade her for days, Agnes.'

'I know one person who'll be pleased — and that's Andrew Neilson.'

Julia set her cup down with a sigh.

'Why? Has he been complaining?' Julia inquired.

'I heard he was anxious to get on with something at the yard. He's done well, Julia.'

176

'He has indeed. I'm most grateful to him. He only did it because he was so worried about Fiona.'

Fiona's eyebrows rose in astonishment. She never ceased to be amazed at people's concern for her. Fancy Andrew Neilson, who she didn't know at all well, worrying about her! And now Agnes, offering to come in twice a day!

'It's awfully good of you.' She turned a smile of deep appreciation to her neighbour. 'But I'm sure I'll be all right.'

'No. I tell you what,' Agnes interrupted. 'Don't you get up in the morning till I come in and give you your breakfast and light the fire.'

'I'll do that before I go!' Julia put in.

'You attend to your work, Julia. We'll manage this end!'

Agnes put her cup down, breathed deeply, and rose to go.

'I'll have to be going. Cheerio, Fiona.'

Julia rose, too, and accompanied her. They went out the back way still arguing about who would do what at Rowanlea.

'I'll just go along with Agnes a bit of the way, Fiona . . . ' Julia called back before closing the door with a soft click behind them.

Fiona smiled. They wouldn't want her to

177

hear their discussion which would be all about saving her any worry. What wonderful friends to her they were!

She picked up her sewing and then put it down again as she saw a car coming up the front drive. It was Andrew Neilson's.

He parked on the gravel and gave the customary knock on the front door before opening it and coming in.

★ ★ ★

'Don't get up,' he greeted her. 'I saw you at the window.'

She looked up at him wondering why on earth he'd come. It would be to see Julia, of course.

'Do sit down,' she said. 'Julia'll be back in a minute. There's tea in the pot. Wait and I'll get you a cup.'

'No. Wait there. I'll fetch a mug from the kitchen.'

While he was getting it, she hunted around in her mind for some priceless gem of conversation, imagining somehow that the man needed to be entertained. Then she realised it was she who was nervous, and there was a calmness and certainty about everything Andrew Neilson did.

He brought his mug of tea and relaxed

with it into the chair Agnes had vacated.

'How are things?' he asked.

She told him of her progress and that she thought Julia would be resuming work on the Monday.

'Oh, that's great!' he exclaimed, and she'd a funny notion that he meant hers and the baby's well-being — more than the fact that he would be released from his uneasy yoke in two days' time.

What an odd man he was!

Her mind was suddenly filled with a picture of them having their last ding-dong argument about the proposed school closure.

'I think the school's going to get a reprieve,' she told him, with no idea why she should want to provoke him again.

'I'm glad,' he said happily and Fiona almost fell back with amazement.

'Don't tease!' Her colour deepened.

'I'm not,' he said earnestly. 'I'm beginning to see what you meant.' His dark eyes, which had danced with amusement, now crinkled into laughter, and she saw again the humour that had been her first impression of him from as long ago as Willie's party.

'What I came about,' he leaned forward suddenly, 'was this. I've seen to it, and there's a grant coming to you from the

Mission Fund, which will tide you over for a while.'

'I'd no idea!' She was incredulous. 'Are you sure? I mean . . . Do I qualify?'

'You do. And you'll find that a useful cheque will come in with the post at the beginning of each month. I hope you'll find that a help.'

'A help! It's like . . . like a miracle! I was getting really worried about ways and means. If only I could have taken a job right away. As it is — ' She shrugged helplessly.

'Don't worry about anything until after the birth . . . When is it?'

'March.'

'Great! He'll arrive with the spring lambs — with the whole summer ahead. Good planning!'

Fiona looked stricken.

'Oh, heavens, I'm sorry!' A look of painful remorse crossed his face. He was silent for a moment, biting his lip, and then he leaned towards her. 'Look. Look at me.'

He held her eyes with an expression of deep compassion in his.

'Listen, Fiona. The Lord will provide!'

She moved uneasily and shrugged her shoulders in an uncomprehending gesture.

'Don't worry about anything. All you have to do is trust,' he went on.

'I can't.' Wistfully she gazed at him, tears threatening in her eyes. 'Everything is so terrible, you see.' She forced her voice over the ache in her throat. 'I can't believe at all. I wish I could!'

★ ★ ★

Tony was already seated in the Cul de Sac when Shona pushed open the door and stood there hesitantly.

Tony stood up and raised his hand and she moved towards him. He took her jacket from her with his normal easy manner and she eased into the seat opposite him, not taking her eyes from his face.

He looked beyond her and studied the coloured glass mural across the rooms as the silence between them grew strained until the welcome interruption of the waitress bringing the menus.

'What would you like to eat?'

'N . . . nothing. I can't — eat,' Shona stammered.

He ordered something for himself, some gateau for Shona in spite of her protests, and two glasses of wine.

It was strange being with Tony like this again. Strange and awful. When he'd taken her jacket from her with the old familiar gesture it had seemed that everything was going to be all right. But now he seemed different. Not relaxed, not easygoing any more . . .

The room had become very busy, and just then a laughing group of young people came in and occupied the last of the places, which appeared to have been reserved for them.

'Somebody's birthday — or engagement party!' Tony observed.

The food came then, and Tony proceeded to eat his in silence.

Shona took up her fork and toyed with her gateau, occasionally pushing some of the creamy concoction into her mouth.

'You said,' she breathed raggedly. 'You said you wanted to talk.'

'We do have to talk. But it's becoming increasingly difficult!'

Suddenly he pushed away his plate.

'Come on!' He stood up and grasped her hand. Taken unawares, a thrill — almost like a pain — shot through her. He waited while she struggled out from her side of the table and there was something like a slow caress in his eyes.

In moments Tony had settled the bill and they were out in the orange-lit, continental-style, cobbled square. He draped her jacket over her shoulders.

'Let's stroll down to the park.'

When they came out of Ashton Lane into University Avenue they found that the balmy night had brought out many strollers. And, when they reached the park, a band was playing light-opera numbers. Strolling quietly and listening to the music, they gained the path beside the river.

It turned out that words weren't really necessary after all. Suddenly they stopped walking and stood side by side, staring at the moving water.

'I missed you!' Tony murmured hoarsely.

'I missed you, too!' Tears filled her eyes.

He turned her towards him.

'Don't cry, please, Shona. I can't stand it! Why did you do it? Why did you go away with him?'

The tears spilled over.

'I don't know. Some kind of madness. Being away from home suddenly made me stupid. I'm sorry.' She gulped. 'I don't know how to tell you how sorry.'

'Maybe it was my fault. I don't believe I quite realised — till you did that — how much it mattered.'

'Tony, don't. I realised in time what a fool I'd been. I'll never, never forgive myself.'

'For going out with him?'

'For hurting you. I don't think I realised

either . . . ' Shona swallowed painfully.

His composure crumpled as he pulled her into his arms and his lips descended on hers. His arms tightened as her lips responded to his in tender, disbelieving surrender. A great load seemed to slip from her shoulders and float away on the wings of the music.

'I love you,' Tony murmured.

Shona drew back in the circle of his arms.

'And I love you,' she told him simply.

'Darling,' he murmured. 'I couldn't live without you.' His eyes were dark now. 'Shona, darling, will you marry me?'

'Tony! Are you sure? Is it not too soon? Are we not too young?'

'Don't you want to marry me?' Tony asked.

'I want to marry you more than anything in the world.' She reached up to kiss him.

'Then let's sit down and I'll tell you all the reasons why we must get married very, very soon, my darling.'

'I'm Not Coping . . . '

'Why have I got two packets of porridge oats?' Julia was unpacking her basket in the schoolhouse kitchen.

'Because one of them is mine.' Fiona neatly fielded the box that Julia shied to her, and put it in her own bag.

'And what else belonging to you has Morag made me carry?'

'A jar of coffee?' Fiona asked, smiling.

'Oh, yes. Here you are. Sit down for a minute. You're not in a hurry, are you?'

'No. I've enjoyed my shopping spree at the village. It's such a fabulous morning!' Fiona exclaimed.

'Glorious for November. It's better than a summer's day.' Julia filled the kettle. As she put down the switch the phone shrilled and she went into the hall to answer it.

Fiona, getting their favourite blue cups out of the dresser, could hear one side of the conversation.

'He's down at the boatyard, Shona . . . Yes, of course I'll get the message to him . . . Christmas! That's not long!

185

I'll try . . . but you know how stubborn he can be.'

There was a longer pause this time, then: 'No. It's no trouble. It'll be pleasant to stroll down there. It's lovely here this morning . . . Right, dear. Yes. I'll see you then. That'll be super. Take care . . . '

'That was Shona.' Julia came back, pushing a strand of hair into place and looking harassed.

'What is it?' Fiona inquired, puzzled.

'She and Tony are coming up tonight. They want to get married at Christmas.'

'Willie'll have a fit!' Fiona looked at her friend with dismay.

'That's what's worrying me,' Julia admitted.

'Sit down, Julia. You need a cup of tea before the ordeal!' Fiona laughed.

'Oh, don't laugh, Fiona!' Julia groaned. 'It's not all that funny!'

Fiona handed Julia her tea with an encouraging smile.

'Oh, thanks, Fiona.' Julia took the cup and drank from it gratefully, then she looked up.

'Fiona, will you do me a favour? Will you walk down to the yard with me? Willie won't make such a production of things if there's someone looking on.'

'Yes, of course I'll walk down with you. I'll enjoy it.'

'Oh, good. I don't feel so bad now that I know I've got some moral support.'

When they reached the yard Andrew and Willie were standing on the jetty, appearing engrossed in their converted fishing boat which lay alongside.

'Just look at them!' Julia exclaimed. 'They've got some ploy on! I wonder what the bottle's for?'

'It looks like a launching ceremony.' Fiona giggled. 'Well, a naming one, maybe, since she's already launched.'

Andrew looked up and caught sight of them. 'My, my! Look at this, Willie! Did you rub a magic ring or something?' He turned to the women. 'Willie was just saying he wished he'd asked you to come and name the boat,' he called.

'You were right, Fiona. Many a true word is spoken in jest,' Julia murmured in an aside.

Willie was grinning like a schoolboy, and waving a bottle of sparkling wine at them.

'Come on! Come on! Julia, will you come and name the boat, 'Mary Stewart' for Mary?'

'Here you are, Julia.' Willie handed her the bottle.

'I've not to throw all this nice stuff away, Willie, have I?' Julia asked in dismay.

'Certainly, you've to smash it. It'll bring her luck. Are we all ready, then?' He looked round gleefully. 'You stand next to me, Fiona.'

Fiona's eyes were merry. 'If we'd known we were coming to a ceremony, we'd have put on fancy hats, wouldn't we, Julia? You might have warned us, Willie!'

'Och, it's just a wee ship, not a Cunard liner.' Willie chortled.

Julia collected herself and stood up straight and solemn.

'Everyone who knew Willie's wife remembers her as a kind, dear friend,' she said in clear, ringing tones. 'So it's with great pride that I name this ship *Mary Stewart* after her. May God bless her and all who sail in her.'

There was a momentary pause during which fond memories misted the eyes of the big, brawny seaman.

Then Julia drew back her arm and let the bottle fly against the bow, where it smashed with a marvellous scrunch.

The men shouted with laughter as the wine foamed all over the dark blue hull, and Fiona clapped enthusiastically.

'Great, Julia. You did that really well. Most royal,' Andrew observed. 'Now,' he swept his arm towards the boat, 'come for a sail with us. Be our first passengers.

188

We're not going to call a halt to this merry party!'

Julia hesitated. 'We came down with a message . . . '

'Oh, come on!' Willie coaxed. 'You can tell us when we're underway. It's a great day for the trials. And it's a good forecast, too!'

Fiona astonished herself by agreeing spontaneously, and they were ceremoniously handed on board, as carefree as young girls.

'Start her up, Andrew,' Willie called as Andrew made for the wheelhouse. 'I want to hear the engine again. She should be fine after the overhaul.'

Julia stuck close to Willie, waiting for her opportunity to relay Shona's message.

'Come into the wheelhouse, Fiona, in case it gets draughty,' Willie invited as the engine throbbed into life and the boat moved slowly away from the jetty. Seagulls swooped low over the deck on a food hunt.

As they reached the open water, Fiona began to feel exhilarated. There was a great sense of freedom and getting-away-from-it-all out here.

Willie stood in the bow looking forward, an expression of pure joy on his face. Julia smiled at his happiness. He looked so relaxed, so at peace. It was truly a marvellous day. The sky was high, transparent azure, and they were sailing over a net of diamonds thrown across the sea.

'It's hot enough for a sunshade!' Fiona popped her head out of the wheelhouse.

Willie turned round. 'Ah. We never thought of an awning, Andrew. Maybe we should think about getting one . . . ' Then suddenly, as if he had just remembered, he turned round to Julia. 'What was it you wanted to tell me, Julia?'

Julia gave a sigh, marshalling her thoughts. 'Shona phoned,' she told him.

'Did she now? And what did she want?'

* * *

There was a pause while Julia tried to chose her words carefully.

'She said to tell you she and Tony are coming up tonight for the weekend. They want to . . . ' She looked down at the toe of her shoe, making circles on the deck. 'They want to get married at Christmas!'

'What?' Willie's face went crimson and he drew himself erect.

'They just wanted to come up and discuss it with you first . . . ' Julia began, desperately trying to calm him down.

'Discuss it, is it? There'll be no discussions!' His mouth twisted. 'She wheedled me into accepting the engagement.' He stamped the deck. 'I forbid this. It's too soon. I won't have it! Phone them and tell them not to bother coming up tonight!'

Julia put her hand on his arm. 'Don't say no yet, Willie,' she pleaded. 'Think about it. What difference will it make?'

He shrugged off her arm.

'No, never!' he shouted so loudly that Fiona swung out of the wheelhouse to come to her friend's rescue.

'You just want to keep Shona your baby for ever, Willie. You're just being selfish!' Julia declared in return.

Fiona wondered what on earth she could do to help the situation.

'Willie,' she said reasonably, 'if you forbid young people to marry nowadays, they're liable to go and live together anyway.'

Andrew, watching the older man carefully, realised that Fiona's efforts weren't helping and decided the best thing to do was head straight back for the shore.

'Fiona!' he called, in order to remove her from the line of fire. 'Come here a minute.'

Gratefully, Fiona beat a retreat. She'd never seen Willie looking so angry.

'What do you want, Andrew?' she asked.

'I need your help.' He grinned at her

encouragingly as she stumbled back into the wheelhouse. 'Willie's going to blow a gasket. We'd better go in.'

Back at the jetty Andrew helped Julia and Fiona ashore, and Willie marched away, leaving him to make the boat fast on his own.

It was the afternoon before Julia saw Willie again. He came up the path as she was brushing a few late leaves off her doorstep. His face was set.

'Can I come in a minute, Julia?' he asked gruffly.

She turned wary eyes on him. 'Yes, Willie. Come away in.'

'Did you phone them?' he asked abruptly, choosing to go into the kitchen.

'No. How could I? They'd have left by now.'

'She's over-young, Julia.' He turned wounded eyes to her.

She waited in silence. She'd been annoyed with him, but now she just wanted to comfort him. He looked so forlorn.

'Ach!' At last he squared his shoulders. 'Ach, Julia, why am I being so daft? I can't keep her my wee girlie for ever. Maybe I'd be best just to let her go, and get it over, eh?'

'Yes, Willie.' She sank down on a chair

at the table as though her legs had lost their power.

He paced to the table and took a seat opposite her. Holding out his hand to her, palm upwards, she couldn't help herself responding by placing hers in it. She wanted to touch him.

His grasp tightened as though he was afraid she'd pull away.

'You'll have to help me.' His voice thickened. 'Julia?'

She swallowed. 'I'll help you all I can, Willie.'

'But will you, Julia? Can you? Enough?' He brought his other hand down on the hand he clasped, imprisoning it. 'You don't know what enough is, yet. You don't know the kind of help I want from you . . . I want you to marry me!'

The words dropped into a pool of silence.

Julia couldn't speak. A flush of colour mounted her cheeks and her eyes began to star with tears. She looked young suddenly.

'Julia — say something! Have I made a fool of myself! Am I too old? Why should we let these young ones have it all their own way? What about us? We're not dead yet!'

His eyes began to sparkle. He lifted his head. His confidence returned.

'Say yes, Julia!' he demanded. 'Say yes — or I'll make you!'

'Willie!' At last Julia was shocked out of her emotional torpor. 'Are you threatening me?'

'Yes!' Willie declared.

She looked into his eyes, love at last shining out of hers.

'Well, how could I say no — after that? You sound quite fierce.'

Relieved, overjoyed, he got up and came round to pull her up into his arms.

'I can be fierce, love. But I can also be gentle. Marry me — and you'll learn just how gentle I can be . . . '

In his warm embrace she felt a sense of being in a safe harbour, and as though, all her life, she'd been coming towards it.

* * *

'Thank goodness there are only two more shopping days till Christmas!' Shona was talking to herself. She flopped down on the only clear space on her bed. Bundles of clothes were heaped arm-high all around her.

When she and Tony had insisted on a Christmas-holiday wedding, they'd completely forgotten that the preceding week would be the most hectic in Shona's year. Customers six-deep at the counter and long, extra hours had drained her.

The doorbell shrilled.

'Who on earth?' Her flatmates were out. She sighed. She'd have to go and answer the door herself. When she threw it open, to a second insistent ringing, her eyes spread wide in amazement.

'Eileen!' She gasped. 'Where on earth did *you* spring from?'

'I thought I'd come and help you pack,' Eileen informed her.

'Help me pack?' A stab of uneasiness shot through Shona. Eileen looked so strained . . .

'Come on in. I'm just going to make a cup of tea.' Shona was guiding Eileen into the kitchen as she talked. 'I thought you said you couldn't get away till the day before the wedding.'

Eileen placed her coat over a chair and her slim body went taut. 'I had to get away from London.'

As Shona switched on the kettle she studied her sister. She looked as though her nerves were at full stretch.

'You're awfully thin, Eileen.'

'You'll have a scraggy bridesmaid!' she joked, but Shona noticed the strain behind her smile.

195

'Nonsense. You'll be so elegant. You'll put the bride in the shade.'

The old warmth between them was seeping back.

'I'll never do that, Shona. You're the beauty!' There was no envy in Eileen's voice, only warmth.

Eileen propped herself on the edge of a stool at the kitchen table while Shona brought the tea.

'What is it, Eileen?' She sounded like the elder sister now.

'I don't know.' Eileen lifted her mug jerkily. 'I . . . I just don't know what's gone wrong with me. Oh, Shona . . . '

Torment looked out of her eyes.

'I'm not coping. My tutor says I'm not giving the new pieces my all. That the magical quality of my work had — has vanished . . . '

There was a long, painful pause as her throat caught and at last she sobbed out brokenly, 'Oh, Shona!' and hot, wet tears ran down her cheeks.

★ ★ ★

Julia and Fiona, both looking extremely elegant, sat among the bride's guests toward the front of the church.

196

Julia turned round when the organist broke into the bridal march.

As they passed, Shona seemed to float down the aisle on her father's arm, Eileen moving gracefully behind.

Shona was all white and gold. Soft white dress and golden hair, gold and pearl necklet, and a bouquet of bronze and yellow flowers. Tony's eyes widened at the vision of her when their glances met.

Eileen's waist is tiny, Julia thought. She's too slim — and some motherly instinct gave her heart a pang.

After the singing of a hymn, the minister began the solemnising of the marriage. Eileen had attended several weddings recently, some in the South, but somehow this time the words of the service penetrated with more than usual significance.

Eileen's thoughts were beginning to unravel. If you loved someone — very much — you would be faithful to them alone, forsaking all other things, perhaps sell everything for that one pearl. At least certain natures would. It might not be right for everyone, but she was beginning to believe that it might be for her.

The ring was given and received. It was almost over. Shona and Tony stood now with hands joined as the minister blessed them.

'The Lord bless you and keep you . . . '

After that a hymn, a benediction, the signing of the register, and they were walking back up the aisle.

Eileen's dress was of amber, and she wore the chain with the ring-charms on it that Duncan had given her when she went away. She saw the guests as a sea of faces. Out of the sea Duncan's face shimmered into focus. Their eyes met. He seemed taller, more rugged, his eyes a more blazing blue, his hair blacker.

She ventured a small, friendly smile. But his face remained impassive. Her heart immediately felt bruised, numbed by the shock of his not smiling back at her. Her expression remained calm, but underneath the soft bodice of her dress her heart hammered painfully.

★ ★ ★

It was, Tony's family declared, the best wedding they'd ever attended. The fun seemed to go on and on. The hotel had produced an excellent meal, and over it they'd listened to the witty Gaelic banter, which reached its peak in the speeches.

Later in the evening, the number of guests

seemed to double, as all the young people from miles around crowded in to attend the evening buffet-dance.

Tony's brothers found plenty of good dancing partners. His eldest brother, Sandy, who'd been the best man, continually partnered Eileen who, all the time, was trying not to let her eyes stray towards Duncan Campbell. He seemed to have attached himself to their old school friend, Jessie McLean.

Eileen felt exhausted suddenly at the end of the dance, and begged Sandy to excuse her. She hastened into the ladies' cloakroom and sank down on to a chair. I've lost him! she wept inwardly.

Just then Jessie McLean entered the cloakroom and went over to the mirror.

'Oh, Eileen! I didn't see you there! It's a lovely wedding! Shona looks beautiful!' she exclaimed.

Eileen felt as though her agony must be showing in her eyes as she and Jessie chattered about the wedding and Shona's plans.

'I'll come back in with you!' She jumped up as Jessie completed drawing vermilion lipstick over her lips.

'Come on, then,' Jessie replied heartily. 'We're sitting over near the bar.'

When they approached him, Duncan was lounging against the small bar. Looking at him directly, Eileen's thoughts swung this way and that. He was lean and hard and his blue eyes were narrowed.

He straightened suddenly. Please don't let him walk away, she implored silently. I'm in love with him and I'd do *anything* to have him love me again!

She tried to be natural and converse as though she'd never been away. She tried to be bright and entertaining. She told a comical story, and was rewarded by a roar of laughter from Duncan.

He'd noted the flush on her cheeks and the rather hectic light in her eyes.

'You're a caution, Eileen!' he declared, when he'd wiped his eyes. Then he resumed his lazy stance, thinking that her figure was even more trim than he remembered.

Sandy came up and claimed Jessie for a dance, and a flicker of relief entered Eileen's eyes. Duncan was watching her. An idea stirred and he veiled his eyes again. Was she? Could she be — jealous? Cool Eileen, jealous of Jessie?

He looked down at her provocatively. She'd hurt him going away like that! She couldn't have it every way!

'Dance?' he asked her, gripping her wrist

200

rather too tightly and swirling her on to the floor.

When she was in his arms she'd a mad desire to stop dancing, to slow down to a complete halt, to put her head on his chest — and just cling there.

Surrounded By Love

Shona and Tony took a respite from dancing and went over to the table where some of Tony's family were seated with Willie, Fiona and Julia.

'I'm glad you're here, Fiona!' Shona exclaimed. 'It's lucky to have an expectant mum at your wedding!'

'Happy to oblige!' Fiona laughed. 'The only trouble is my partners having to push two of us round the floor!'

In the midst of the laughter Andrew approached and asked Fiona to dance.

'No, Andrew. Thank you. That last dance is the last I'm having till after March!' She laughed again, ending on a small dry cough.

'Sit down, Andrew. You're needing a rest yourself,' Willie teased. 'Where's your glass? Pass the bottle, Julia.'

'Please?' Julia prompted.

'In the name . . . ' Willie groaned.

'Right, Dad!' Shona leaned her hands on his shoulders. 'You just say, 'please.' You might as well get into practice now, for when you two get married.'

'When's your wedding to be?' Tony's mother asked.

'Easter,' Willie told her. 'We have to wait for a school holiday. Julia's the school-teacher here, you see.'

'Will you go on teaching after you marry, Julia?' Shona wanted to know. 'I should warn you that Dad could be a full-time job! Or — ' a thought struck her ' — is the school to be closing anyway?'

'No! It's not!' Fiona and Andrew chorused in unison, before Julia had time to answer.

'We've won!' Fiona beamed. 'The school's to remain open.'

'Oh, that's great!' Shona clapped her hands. 'Great news!'

'And it's largely thanks to Fiona's campaigning!' Andrew declared.

'It often takes an incomer to see what's to be done,' someone said tactlessly.

'Fiona's not an 'incomer'!' Willie said loudly and warmly, reaching over for her hand. 'Fiona is one of us!'

Fiona squeezed Willie's hand, feeling a sudden rush of love for them all.

Julia thought the atmosphere was getting a bit overcharged, so she answered Shona's question.

'I — I mean we — haven't decided yet what I'll do. I'll go on till the summer at least. I would have to give quite a bit of notice anyway.' She turned to Fiona. 'I might keep the job warm for you, Fiona. Did you ever fancy that?'

Fiona looked thoughtful. 'I'll certainly have to work for my living. It's a thought, Julia. If you decide to leave — I could maybe, at least, apply . . . '

'Is the asthma still troubling you, Fiona?' Willie enquired.

'D'you know — it's so much better, Willie! It's great. The doctor's amazed. He swears it's the relaxation exercises.' Her smile lit up her face. Pregnancy and returning health had brought a new glow to Fiona.

The bridal couple and some of the guests were spending the night in the hotel. It was lucky because, when the festivities ended, the snow was falling.

'It doesn't matter. It never lies here, anyway,' the residents kept telling visitors, as snow continued to fall.

'What about the roads?'

'Och, well, we'll not be talking about contingencies until they happen,' was the cheerful local philosophy.

Various groups of young people were making off for chosen houses to continue ceilidhing till morning.

Eileen, Jessie and Duncan came out into

the falling snow together. Their intention was to go on to one of the ceilidhs with their closest friends.

But suddenly Eileen felt stupified with exhaustion. Full of anecdotes, laughing, brittle, she had played for Duncan's attention all evening. He must know she had. Sometimes, as he'd danced with her, she'd thought . . . Oh, it didn't matter. I must have made myself so obvious, she thought wearily.

Now, she felt she couldn't go on.

'I'll have to go home,' she announced lamely.

The others turned to stare at her in astonishment. It was unheard of.

'I must,' she insisted. 'I'm dead beat!' She turned towards her home. 'Goodnight!' she called, breaking into a tripping run.

'Come on!' Jessie caught Duncan's arm and pulled him towards his car. 'Let's hurry. I'm cold!'

Eileen knew she just had to get home. All she wanted now was oblivion. Her father was escorting Julia and Fiona to the schoolhouse. He'd most likely stay there for ages.

When Eileen reached their living-room, she kicked off her high-heeled, narrow-strapped sandals and, too tired even to go upstairs, she flopped into her father's chair.

'Eileen!'

She started awake. Her eyes flew open. She didn't know she'd been asleep. Somehow Duncan was standing in the room, the snow melting on his black hair and the shoulders of his dark jacket.

'Eileen,' he repeated softly.

He closed the room door behind him without turning round, and then leaned against it. He didn't move, but his eyes were compelling as they held hers. He moved not a step nearer to her, but suddenly he opened his arms wide.

She felt a deep thrill of responding desire, left the chair as though in a dream, and flew across the room to home right into his tight embrace. As they clung together, they tried to speak.

'I might have kept up my show of indifference all night — if you'd come to the ceilidh. But — because you weren't there . . . ' Duncan's cold front was gone. 'Because you weren't there — after seeing you again . . . realising . . . '

'Duncan. I can't live my life without you. I can't manage . . . It was as though someone had switched off the sun. I felt cold, and lonely, and unable to enjoy myself.'

'That's the way it's been ever since you went away.' With a groan, he covered her mouth with his.

Ages later he dragged his lips away and looked down at her, his eyes concerned. 'But your music, Eileen?'

'It's gone to pieces.' A trembling sigh escaped her. 'I couldn't get it together, I was so unhappy away from you. I only just discovered what was wrong with me.'

'We've a lot to discuss,' he said softly, eagerly.

'I know. I've a lot to tell you. But, not now, Duncan ... Let it wait till the morning. I just want you to hold me. I'm so terribly — tired.'

★ ★ ★

'You shouldn't have come out in this!' Dr Ian Frazer took Willie's wrist and felt for his pulse.

'Ach, I couldn't be bringing you along, Ian.' Willie gave an involuntary shiver, although he was finding the surgery an oasis of warmth and brightness after coming through the murky February weather.

'It's always in the New Year we get it.' The doctor squinted at the window, black, speckled with the flakes sliding down it.

'Aching all over, are you?'

'Ay.'

'I can't remember when we had such a heavy fall.' Willie's throat was being examined. 'Painful to swallow?'

The assent was a croak.

'It's a pretty virulent flu that's on the go, Willie,' the doctor told him. 'I think it'd be best if you went home to bed and stayed there till I get round to see you.'

'I'll take a hot toddy,' Willie told him.

'It won't cure you.' The doctor smiled. 'But it might comfort. Take soluble aspirins and fluids and tell Julia to feed you soup or gruel. Be sure and keep your strength up.'

Willie sighed thankfully when, finally, he laid his aching head on the pillow and dragged the bedclothes up to his chin. His throat was raw and evil demons were drilling a road through his skull. Ach! He would just have to put up with it!

Julia decided that she'd have to let the school out early when relatives, as though warned by radar, began arriving to steer the children home.

Julia, in wellingtons, stood in the middle of the road until she'd satisfied herself that every last child had an escort. She watched them pass through the paths of light streaming from the houses, before going back to lock up the school.

She decided to go then to see how Willie had got on at the doctor's, before getting herself indoors for the night.

She found him, looking faintly blue, a miserable figure huddled in bed in a cold room. She switched on the light and the electric fire and closed the curtains.

'The light's hurting my eyes.' Willie moaned. So she worked by the firelight; administering the aspirin, tidying and smoothing the bed, fetching him an extra pillow, and generally making him more comfortable.

He tried to give her a smile of thanks, but it was a shadow of his normal cheerful grin.

'In half an hour I'll bring you some soup and bread. That'll give the aspirin time to work and you'll find it easier to swallow.'

Willie wanted to say that he didn't want food and he couldn't swallow anyway, but it was too much effort and he remained dumb.

He looked so wretched that Julia felt impelled to caress his tousled head for a moment, like she would a troubled small boy. Then she went away to prepare some food for the invalid.

Fiona saw the snow deepening all around Rowanlea and suspected that she was becoming cut off from her friends. Never mind, she consoled herself, they're always telling me it never lasts so near the sea. All the same, I think I'll just fetch in a few more logs in case it gets too deep in the yard.

She made two trips to the woodshed, her gumboots getting clogged with snow. She was nearing the door with her second load when her feet shot from under her, and she went down on her back with a tremendous thump.

She lay for a moment, completely winded, wondering how she was going to get up. Eventually she managed to roll round on to her hands and knees and push herself upright again. She retrieved the scattered logs, stumbled indoors and deposited them with the others.

Better make a cup of tea, she ordered herself, filling the kettle with hands that trembled, and then she rubbed away the involuntary tears that were squeezing out of her eyes.

'Brian?' she enquired wistfully, uselessly, her words fading into the surrounding silence.

She perked up after she had had her tea,

sitting toasting her legs at the fire. And when, later, Agnes arrived carrying some peats that she'd gathered as she'd passed the shed, she was greeted with a glad smile.

★ ★ ★

'Agnes! How lovely! You shouldn't have come out in this!'

'The phone-line is down,' Agnes announced, shaking out her coat and scarf and hanging them on the back of the kitchen door. 'How are you?'

'I'm fine!' Fiona wriggled her stockinged toes in the firelight and pushed a strand of hair behind her ear. 'Come and sit down,' she said eagerly. 'How on earth did you manage over?'

'I came by the fields and the footbridge. The wind has blown it a bit thinner there. How long is it till the baby is due now?' She stretched her hands towards the blaze.

'Not for another three or four weeks,' Fiona informed her.

'Oh?' Agnes gave a relieved sigh. 'That's fine then. This snow will be gone by the morning. Now, is there anything you need? Duncan's putting chains on the pick-up, and he'll be over to clear your yard.' Her head bobbed confidently. 'Don't get up, Fiona. I can get a cup for myself.'

Fiona sank back gratefully.

'You're looking fine.' Agnes came back with her cup and the teapot. She refilled Fiona's cup, set the pot on the hearth, and settled down for a blether.

Fiona enjoyed her visitor's company and was sorry when she gave the time-honoured signal for departure.

'Well, I'd better away, Fiona,' Agnes declared, 'and not keep you back.'

Agnes emptied the teapot, washed the cups, and polished up the sink before getting into her outdoor things again.

'Don't go out at all, Fiona,' were her parting words. 'Duncan will be over in the morning. Just you stay by the fire.'

Unable to contact Fiona by phone, Julia arrived up late the following afternoon. She found Fiona pacing up and down the living-room, her hands at the base of her spine and her face drawn.

'What's the matter, dear?' Julia hurriedly removed her coat and gloves.

'Nothing.' Fiona laughed slightly. 'I slipped outside last night. I didn't think so at the time, but I must have hurt my back. It'll go away. It's nothing.'

Julia could hear a wheezy indrawn breath. 'I don't think you're very well, darling. Is the asthma back, too?'

'A little. Probably with worrying about this.'

Julia left after a brief visit, saying she had to get Willie his tea, but more urgently to contact the doctor as the line to Fiona's house and the Campbells' was still down.

Andrew Neilson was clearing Willie's path when she got back to the village.

'Were you up at Rowanlea, Julia? How's the road?'

'The shore road's been cleared, but I had to walk up to the croft. Fiona's not very well.' Julia hurried past Andrew, into the house and straight to the phone.

Andrew followed her to the door and heard her explain to the doctor's wife about Fiona.

'Is the doctor out?' he queried, when she'd hung up.

'Yes. Old Mrs Stirling's fallen and fractured her leg. It was a tumble Fiona took — going out for logs. That's what started this. She's wheezing and her back is sore.'

'Out for logs! Julia, surely she didn't need to do that!' Andrew was aghast. 'I'll away up and fetch in enough peat and logs to last a siege!' He threw a last shovelful of snow from the path on to the buried lawn, propped the shovel against the wall, and thumped his gloved hands together.

'Willie's been listening to the weather forecast as usual. He tells me there's another blizzard on its way. Will you be up later?'

'Tell her I'll be up as soon as I've given Willie something to eat.' She watched Andrew drive off, noting the crunch of chains. He'll be able to drive right up to the house, she thought.

* * *

'I was wanting to go to Inverness today,' Andrew attempted to distract Fiona with some idle chatter. 'But there's a drift as big as a bus across the loch road — and I couldn't get out to the Inverness road.'

'The snow ploughs will be on their way,' Fiona said more brightly than she felt.

'Yes, but it's taking them all their time to keep the main roads clear. We're just a wee bit isolated at times like this.'

He was outside wielding a shovel again, when the doctor arrived. He examined Fiona in the downstairs bedroom and then came to the door looking very grave.

'Andrew!' He called the other man over. 'Fiona was to go to Inverness at the end of next week, but this baby's in a hurry. Maybe it was the fall she took. I don't know. He's decided to arrive early. She's going into labour.'

Andrew and he went into the living-room while they talked.

'And she's a bit wheezy,' the doctor went on. He squinted out of the window at the sky, made dark by the sudden onslaught of the fresh blizzared from the north-east. 'I wonder if we could get her to Inverness in time?'

Julia arrived in time to hear Andrew's reply.

'We couldn't get her to Inverness at all, Ian. The road's completely blocked.'

Julia's heart sank.

'What'll we do?' She guessed what the emergency was.

The doctor paced up and down the room slapping one fist into the other palm.

'She really needs to be where all the equipment is to hand and there's a nursing team. The baby'll be premature and might need the kind of care only a hospital can provide. Helicopter?'

'They'll all be grounded in this,' Andrew declared. 'Broadford's the only hope.'

'Over the sea to Skye!' Julia quipped, trying to lighten the atmosphere.

'First births are supposed to go to Inverness.' The doctor rubbed his forehead tiredly. 'But maybe — since it's an emergency. They're very skilled there. What's the coast road like, Andrew? It's mighty hazardous at the best of times.'

'The snow doesn't lie the same on the coast road, and I've got chains on. It's the black ice on these narrow, twisting roads that's the worst problem, as you know, Ian.'

'You mean, you would take her?' the doctor asked.

'Yes, if it's the best thing to be done. I'll take her. You can't leave your patients. Of course I'll go.'

Ian Frazer placed his arm on Andrew's shoulder. 'It would be a great relief to me if they would take her at Broadford. I'll see if I can contact them. Maybe they could have an ambulance down at the ferry. Is her case packed, Julia?'

'I'll just go and check everything, Ian.'

★ ★ ★

The journey to Kyle of Lochalsh was a nightmare. The wind-screen wipers worked frantically for about half an hour until the blizzard abated a little. Perhaps a helicopter could have made it now, Andrew thought, but there was no going back.

There was no light but the car's headlights, and it was impossible to guess where the edges of the road were. While Andrew kept the car travelling on the crest, dredging his memory for the contours of the road, his anxiety for Fiona increased.

After what seemed endless more miles, Andrew could see the lights of Kyle and a pain crept up on Fiona. As it grew in intensity she couldn't stop moaning slightly. His attention switched to her involuntarily. The car skidded, the nearside wheels went over the verge, and they came to a shuddering halt.

Although the pain finally faded, her feeling of depression seemed to get worse, increased by the sense that she was alone; that even Andrew had left her side; that he was running towards the lights of Kyle. She lost consciousness.

Much later she became aware that someone was helping her to breathe, that there was an oxygen mask over her face and that she was in an ambulance.

Later still, she was being wheeled on a stretcher and even later — twenty-four hours later — the baby was born. It was a girl.

Overwhelmed with gratitude towards the doctor and nurses who'd helped her over the long hours, Fiona lay exhausted.

The hospital staff had been wonderful, the only thing was that she'd felt so alone. She'd longed for Julia. Even Eileen or Agnes would have done — or Willie or Andrew. She marvelled at how she was thinking about them all — as if they were her family.

★ ★ ★

A member of staff came in then accompanied by another person. They came across to her bed. She was too tired to open her eyes.

'She's asleep,' said the staff-member. 'She's going to be all right. Thank you for waiting. We were rather worried.'

'I wouldn't have left her,' the stranger whispered.

It was Andrew.

She'd never been alone. Andrew had been there waiting all that time. He really was an exceptional man. She must ask him sometime to tell her all that had happened. He must somehow have summoned the ambulance to come and save her — her life and her little daughter's.

'Come and see the baby,' he was invited. 'She's tiny, but perfect. We'll keep them both here until they're stronger. Can you come back later?'

'I've a friend in Broadford. I'll stay there for

218

a few hours, get shaved and have some sleep. And then I'll come back.' Their footsteps faded.

Fiona was drifting, drifting on a cottonwool cloud. Her strength would return. She sensed that she wasn't to worry. She wasn't alone. She'd never been alone. She mustn't sleep, though, just yet. There was something she had to think about.

I have been surrounded, all the time, she mused, by love and help. And now I feel such peace. I've never felt such peace before. Gratitude welled up in her.

When she woke again, Andrew was sitting beside the bed.

'Hello!' he said as her eyes focused on him.

'Hello!' She turned towards him, struggling on to her elbow. She studied his face, the compassion in his eyes arresting her.

'Have you seen the baby, Andrew?'

He nodded, smiling. 'She's perfect.'

A slow, special, new-mother smile curved her lips.

'How kind you are, Andrew — not just bringing me here — but waiting all this time.'

'I wouldn't have left you.'

Andrew's shyness touched her heart. What a good friend he had been to her. In fact, everyone in the village had rallied round when she had needed friendship and understanding.

'You're all so kind — so committed and involved.' She gazed at him with an unusual depth of feeling in her eyes.

Andrew looked embarrassed.

'Achnacraig has changed me in so many ways,' Fiona said softly, tears of emotion filling her eyes.

'How do you mean?'

'Do you remember the arguments we've had about your faith, Andrew — and how I was unable to share it?'

'Yes. I remember.'

'Well, just yesterday, today — I've surprised myself. Thinking about the beauty of our surroundings, the sheer goodness of the people I've met, well, I'm actually beginning to believe what you believe. I now agree with most of what you say.'

'That's great, Fiona. I'm happy for you.'

'Thanks, Andrew.' She looked at him with direct eyes. 'And that's why I want you to be the first to know that I want to have my daughter christened.'

She saw the happiness spring into his eyes, and felt him take her hand in his and press it wordlessly.

* * *

'It's so glorious here in summer,' Shona said, waving a hand at the blue sky. 'You'd think there had never been ice and snow all over the place. Brr . . . '

'You're a proper townie,' Tony teased her, relieving her of her empty glass. She wore a suit of her favourite powder-blue and her groomed hair shone like gold in the sunshine. He never tired of looking at her.

They were all at Rowanlea. The baby had been christened that morning in church, and lay sleeping in her pram in the garden, oblivious to the chatter of the well-wishers gathered all around her.

The minister and his wife were talking to Dr and Mrs Frazer, sitting on chairs under a tree.

'You'd think Julia and Willie had always been together,' remarked Mrs Frazer. 'They look so comfortable in each other's company.'

'It's not good for man to live alone . . . ' quoted the minister, as Andrew brought a tray of savouries to their table.

'Fiona's gone to get more coffee,' he told them. 'That was a moving service you gave us, Reverend. Wasn't the baby good?'

'Julia-Ann is a perfect child,' put in the lady of the manse. 'I'm afraid we're all going to spoil her. I'm for ever making excuses to come up here — and for ever meeting some of the others just leaving!'

'Me!' Mrs Frazer laughed. 'I could cuddle her all day long.'

'Except when Julia's making a prior claim, being the baby's godmother!' Andrew chuckled. 'Of course, you all realise that it's only for me she stops crying if she's hungry!'

'What conceit!' Eileen said. She and Duncan had strolled from the lower lawn in time to catch the last remark. 'I'm sure she'd stop for me,' she added.

'I wish she'd wake up,' she confided in Duncan as the progressed towards the buffet table.

'Eileen.' He put his arm round her and whispered in her ear. 'Make up your mind quickly about our wedding date. This time next year we could be having the party — and you could be cuddling babies for the rest of your life if you wanted to.'

Eileen laughed and flushed. 'That would fairly put up the school roll! That's what you want, isn't it?' She slipped out of his encircling arm. 'Excuse me, Duncan. I must just give Julia a hand.'

'Tell me tonight?'

'I promise!'

★ ★ ★

Agnes Campbell had been telling Shona about the wintry night when Julia-Ann had been born.

'They were over a month in the hospital,' she concluded. 'And, ever since, Fiona hasn't had an asthma attack once.'

'She's like a new person,' Duncan confirmed, just as Fiona came out of the door carrying a large jug of coffee.

She gave it to a young girl who'd come up from the hotel to help her, and came and joined them.

'We're just saying how well you've been since the baby came,' Agnes told her.

Fiona widened her smile and there was a new radiance about her. 'I daren't be ill,' she declared. 'I haven't time!'

Shona looked at her a second time. She was quite beautiful, and Shona new beauty when she saw it. Her skin was clear and glowing, her hair a shining cloud. Her huge eyes, anxious when they'd met first, then haunted, were at peace.

A small wail from the pram was a signal for all the baby's admirers to become alert.

Eileen, speedily leaving her father and Julia, reached the pram first and tenderly lifted the baby. But the crying continued.

Eventually Andrew abandoned the lemonade jug he was wielding and approached; and Eileen, with a rueful smile, surrendered the baby to him. The crying promptly stopped and everyone laughed.

Shona once again, glanced at Fiona, who was serenely enjoying the scene with others. Is that what having a child does for one, she wondered.

'Please excuse me,' Fiona said at last, after they'd watched Andrew carry the baby round, showing her off to her guests. 'I'll have to go and feed her.'

Julia-Ann was sitting up in Andrew's arms, bright eyed and alert. When Fiona reached up to take her, somebody took a snapshot.

It turned out to be one of those rare snaps which shows everyone at their best and looking completely natural. Copies of it were to appear on desks and mantels for many days to come.

Andrew is putting the baby into her mother's arms, and they are surrounded by all their friends. Everybody is smiling at them.

Fiona and her baby, not merely accepted — but cradled at the very heart of Achnacraig.

McLEAN AT THE GOLDEN OWL
George Goodchild
Inspector McLean has resigned from Scotland Yard's CID and has opened an office in Wimpole Street. With the help of his able assistant, Tiny, he solves many crimes, including those of kidnapping, murder and poisoning.

KATE WEATHERBY
Anne Goring
Derbyshire, 1849: The Hunter family are the arrogant, powerful masters of Clough Grange. Their feuds are sparked by a generation of guilt, despair and ill-fortune. But their passions are awakened by the arrival of nineteen-year-old Kate Weatherby.

A VENETIAN RECKONING
Donna Leon
When the body of a prominent international lawyer is found in the carriage of an intercity train, Commissario Guido Brunetti begins to dig deeper into the secret lives of the once great and good.